Dawn and the Halloween Mystery

Dawn and the Halloween Mystery
Ann M. Martin

AN
APPLE
PAPERBACK

SCHOLASTIC INC.
New York Toronto London Auckland Sydney

*The author gratefully acknowledges
Ellen Miles
for her help in
preparing this manuscript.*

ISBN 0-590-48232-7

12 11 10 9 8 7 6 5 4 3 2 1   4 5 6 7 8 9/9

Printed in the U.S.A.   40

First Scholastic printing, October 1994

CHAPTER 1

"Huge muscles," said Jeff. "I mean, really *huge*. Like, *this* big!" He held his hands apart to show me. "And a totally gruesome mask."

"And all in red, right?" I asked, grinning. "Or did you change that to purple?"

"I think I've decided on green," said Jeff, after deliberating for a second. "Green is the most monsterish."

My younger brother Jeff is ten, and if anybody knows what makes a monster monsterish, it's him. He and I were sitting at the kitchen table that October afternoon, eating the nachos our housekeeper, Mrs. Bruen, had prepared for an after-school snack, and talking about Jeff's Halloween costume. He had a sketchpad in front of him, and he was drawing costume ideas with his markers.

My name's Dawn Schafer. I'm a little old for trick-or-treating — I'm thirteen, and in the eighth grade — but Jeff still gets really excited about it. He loves to create elaborate costumes, and he and his friends spend hours making game plans about which neighborhoods to visit for the best "booty." When the trick-or-treating is over, Jeff carefully counts and organizes his loot, and then he hoards it, eating only a little bit each day in order to make it last.

Sometimes, when he's feeling extra generous, he offers me a Snickers bar or a pack of Sweet-Tarts, but I always turn him down. I can't stand junk food, candy included. I don't mind if *he* eats it once in a while. That's his business. (He usually eats pretty healthy stuff.) But I hate the idea of putting refined sugars and weird chemicals in my body.

"What was the best Halloween costume you ever had?" Jeff asked, helping himself to a nacho. A long string of cheese stretched between the nacho and the plate, and Jeff carefully reeled it in and piled it on top of his chip.

I thought for a minute. "I guess it would have to be Pippi Longstocking," I said, smiling at the memory. "I must have been about seven or eight. Mom braided my hair and put wires in it so it stuck straight out, and we painted freckles all over my nose. And I wore this hilarious-looking pair of Dad's shoes. You know how Pippi always wears those big shoes?"

"What was I that year?" Jeff asked.

"You were a mouse," I said.

Jeff made a face. "A *mouse*? How nerdy."

"No, you were cute," I said. "You were a totally adorable little mouse. Don't you remember? You've seen the pictures. Mom must have shot a whole roll of us in those costumes."

"Oh, yeah," said Jeff.

Then, all of a sudden, we both stopped talking. The only noise in the house came from the living room, where Mrs. Bruen was vacuuming. I could guess what Jeff was thinking about, because it was probably pretty close to what I was thinking about. We were both "seeing" those pictures: a young Dawn, with the same long, pale blonde hair and blue eyes, and an even younger Jeff, with matching blue eyes and that familiar, funny cowlick in his hair.

Our eyes and hair are still the same, but everything else has changed since those pictures were taken.

"That was a long time ago, Jeff," I said gently.

"It sure was," said Jeff, looking sad. "Sometimes it's hard to remember what it was like when Mom and Dad were still together."

Our parents are divorced. For now, Jeff and

I are both living with my dad in the town where we grew up: Palo City, California. That's outside of Anaheim, where Disneyland is. My mom lives in Stoneybrook, Connecticut, which is where *she* grew up, and where our grandparents, Granny and Pop-Pop, still live. Jeff and I both moved out to Connecticut with Mom after the divorce, but Jeff never adjusted to life in the East. He ended up coming back here to live with our dad.

I adjusted to Connecticut just fine. I made tons of friends, partly because I joined this cool club called the BSC (or Baby-sitters Club), which I'll explain more about later, and one *best* friend. Her name's Mary Anne Spier, and now she's my stepsister, too, because my mom married her dad!

Anyway, while I did love living in Connecticut, I also found that I missed Jeff and my dad tremendously. That's why I decided to come back out here and live with them for awhile.

Now, being in California again has been pretty wonderful. I belong to a club here, too: it's called the We ♥ Kids Club, and all my best California friends are in it, including my *oldest* best friend, Sunny Winslow. She and I grew up together. I love our house out here: it's all on one floor, built around a courtyard, and it has these long, cool, tiled halls and skylights in every room. Sunny calls it *Casa Schafer*. (That just means "Schafer House," in Spanish.) Mrs. Bruen keeps the house spotless, and she's also a wonderful cook. My school is great. And I've even grown to like Carol, this woman my dad is engaged to. (We had our ups and downs at first, to put it mildly.)

But.

You knew there was a "but" coming, didn't you?

Here it is: *But* even though I love California, I am not totally, totally happy here. I miss my mom like crazy, and I hate being away from Mary Anne and my other friends in the BSC. So, I know it won't be long before I go back to Connecticut to live. And of course, when I do, I'll miss everybody out here!

Being a divorced kid is never easy. For me, it means my life is always like a puzzle with one lost piece. It means I'm always missing somebody or someplace.

I don't mean to complain. The truth is, there's a good side to my bi-coastal life. I have two sets of wonderful friends, two great houses to live in (the one in Stoneybrook is an old, old farmhouse that's probably haunted!), and two parents who are probably happier now than they were when they were together. That's a whole lot more than some people have!

"Papier-mâché?" Jeff asked, interrupting my thoughts.

"What?" I asked.

"Do you think I should build the muscles out of papier-mâché?" He showed me the sketch he'd been making.

"Foam rubber might be easier," I said, turning the sketch to look at it. "You could stuff your costume with it."

"Great idea!" Jeff said. He took the sketch back and started to draw some nasty-looking fangs on the mask he was planning.

Mrs. Bruen bustled into the kitchen. "Hi, kids," she said. "How are the nachos?"

"Terrific," I said. "Thanks!"

"Glad you like them." She reached into a closet, pulled out a sweater, and threw it over her shoulders. "I'll see you both tomorrow," she said.

"How's Nicholas?" I asked. Nicholas is Mrs. Bruen's newest grandson. She's spending a lot of time at her daughter's house lately, helping to take care of him.

"Oh, he's a little charmer," she answered. "Did I tell you he's cutting his first tooth?" She shook her head. "They grow up so fast," she murmured. Then she smiled at me, waved, and headed out the door.

Mrs. Bruen's been working at our house less lately, partly because of her grandson but partly because we don't need her help as much these days. Why? Because Carol's around all the time, and she helps out a lot with the cooking and cleaning up.

Carol. I should tell you more about her, because she's becoming a pretty important person in my life. In fact, soon she'll be my *stepmother*! That's kind of hard to imagine, because Carol really isn't a motherly type. In fact, even though she's a grown-up, I think she may be *cooler* than me. She has cool clothes and a cool haircut and she drives a cool red sports car, and she knows all about the coolest new groups, since she loves to watch MTV.

At first I wasn't thrilled by my dad's hip girlfriend. I think I felt a little jealous of Carol. Okay, I felt a *lot* jealous. Ready for a confession? When Dad and Carol got engaged the first time, I freaked out. I went so bananas that I actually bought myself a plane ticket and flew back to Connecticut without telling a soul!

That didn't go over too well with *either* of my parents.

I was back in California before I'd even gone through jet lag, and I did a lot of thinking during the zillions of hours of baby-sitting it took to earn enough money to pay my dad back for that plane ticket. Ever since then I've tried to be more accepting of my dad's relationship with Carol. Lately it's been easier, because I've discovered that I actually like her. Especially compared to some of the *other* women my dad dated during a time when he and Carol were on the outs.

Anyway, by now Carol has become a regular at *Casa* Schafer. She's here for dinner, oh, probably four nights a week. She and my dad cook together a lot, and Jeff and I get stuck with the dishes (which I really don't mind all that much). She helps Jeff with his math homework, and sometimes she shows me things I can do with my hair, such as make these awesome braids I'd always wanted. When we watch movies on the VCR, Carol always sits on the green couch, next to my dad. That's, like, *her* spot now. She's definitely becoming part of the family.

Lately, Carol and my dad have been talking a lot about wedding plans. They haven't made too many decisions yet, even though they're getting married in December, but I do know that I'm going to be a bridesmaid and Jeff will be the best man. We're both pretty psyched about it.

That night, Carol came over just as my dad arrived home from work. Jeff showed them the plans for his costume. "Whoa!" said Carol, pretending to be scared.

"Love it," said Dad. Then he turned to me. "How about you, Sunshine? What are you going to be?" Sunshine is his pet name for me.

"Oh, Dad," I said. "I'm too old for that stuff."

He sighed. "I remember when you used to get so excited about Halloween," he said. "I guess my little girl is growing up. Do you remember when you dressed up like that book character? Pippa Longsocks?"

"Pippi *Longstocking*," I said, laughing. "I do remember. I was just telling Jeff about that."

Dad looked at both of us fondly, and I could tell he was conjuring up that same batch of pictures we'd been thinking about earlier. "You guys are a treat to come home to," he said, sounding a little choked up. Then he smiled. "And speaking of treats, look what I brought home for dessert!" He showed us a white bag with red writing.

"Apple-raisin turnovers?" I said. "From the Natural Baker?" He nodded. "All *right*!"

That night, after a dinner of Carol's favorite vegetable chimichangas (she cooked) and those outrageous turnovers for dessert, I wrote a short letter to Mary Anne:

Dear Mary Anne,

I've been thinking about Halloween in Stoneybrook, and how it's like something out of a storybook. The chill in the air, the pumpkins, the piles of leaves to shuffle through, the smell of woodsmoke.... It's not the same in California, where the palm trees are green all year round. But the kids here get just as excited as the kids there.

Is the BSC planning anything special for Halloween? I'd love to hear about it if you are. Meanwhile, W/B/S. I miss you like crazy.

Love, Dawn

P.S. Please give my mom a big hug for me. I miss her like crazy, too!

CHAPTER 2

"So then, right as class was ending, I finally figured out what Tom Swanson's eyebrows have always reminded me of," said Sunny, giggling. "You know how dark and bristly they are? Well, I guess I was staring at them, and then all of a sudden it came to me and I started to crack up. *Caterpillars!* They look just like a couple of wiggly caterpillars sitting there on his forehead!"

We all cracked up. Tom Swanson is somebody I've known since first grade, and now that Sunny mentioned it, I could see exactly what she meant about his eyebrows.

It was Wednesday afternoon, and my friends — Sunny, Maggie, and Jill — and I were hanging out at Sunny's house, eating five-grain tortilla chips with freshly made organic salsa. Every once in a while the phone would ring, and one of us would answer it. For example, it rang in the middle of our laughing fit about Tom Swanson, and since I was the first one to catch my breath, I grabbed it. After listening for a moment, I put my hand over the receiver. "It's Mrs. DeWitt. I mean, Cynthia. Anybody want to sit for Erick and Ryan on Sunday?"

Maggie reached for the record book. "It's hard to tell, with all these crossouts," she said, "but it looks like you're the only one free, Dawn."

"Okay," I said. I took my hand off the receiver and told Mrs. DeWitt (lately she's insisted on being called Cynthia, but I keep forgetting) that I'd be there at four.

That's how we arrange baby-sitting jobs in the We ♥ Kids Club. I guess you could call our get-together a meeting, but it wasn't much like the meetings we have in my *other* baby-sitting club back in Connecticut, the BSC.

When I first returned to California and the We ♥ Kids Club invited me to be a temporary member, I was shocked at how laid-back they were about running meetings. But now I'm not only used to it — I *like* it. I just hope I don't act this casual back in Stoneybrook during a BSC meeting. Kristy would have a cow.

Kristy Thomas, that is. She's the president of the BSC, and the one who thought up the idea for it. And since the California club is based (sort of) on the Connecticut club, maybe

I should explain a little about the BSC first.

The BSC grew out of an idea of Kristy's. She guessed that parents would love being able to call one number to arrange for a responsible sitter. Her guess was right, and the club has been successful from the start. Here's how it works: the BSC meets three afternoons a week, from five-thirty to six, and parents can call during those times to set up jobs. The club secretary keeps track of everyone's schedules in a record book, so when calls come in she can check to see who's available. Kristy also dreamed up the club notebook, where members record their sitting experiences for everyone to read, so that they know what's going on with the regular clients. The club treasurer keeps track of how much money everyone earns, and also collects dues to help pay for things such as the phone bill (the phone belongs to the vice-president, and the club meets in her room).

It's all very organized — unlike the We ♥ Kids Club, which has no officers, no treasury, and no club notebook. The We ♥ Kids Club recently began keeping a record book and having one regular meeting a week, but only because we got really, really busy after a local TV station did a story on us. (Kristy was pretty jealous about our brush with fame!)

Kristy makes a terrific club president because she's full of energy and great ideas. She's also used to dealing with groups of people, since she has a large — and complicated — family. She and her three brothers (two older and one younger) grew up with only their mom to take care of them, after their dad walked out on the family. Then, her mom got married again, to this humongously rich guy who has two kids, a boy and a girl, from his first marriage. (They live at Kristy's house part-time.) Once they were married, Kristy's mom and stepdad decided to adopt a little girl together. Then Kristy's grandmother moved in, too. Now they all live happily in a gigantic mansion, along with an assortment of pets.

The club secretary is Mary Anne Spier, my best friend (and stepsister). Mary Anne is also Kristy's best friend, and while the two of them look a little alike (they're both on the short side, with brown eyes and brown hair), they have very different personalities. Mary Anne is shy and sensitive, and more of a listener than a talker. (She is also *completely* lovable, and the best sister I could have asked for.) Her mom died not long after Mary Anne was born, and her dad brought her up on his own. Until, that is, he got back together with my mom, whom he had dated when they were both in high school. (As Mary Anne would say with a sigh, "It's *such* a romantic story!")

Mary Anne has a boyfriend named Logan Bruno, who manages to be both a regular kind of guy and the sweetest person in the world. He's an associate member of the BSC, which means he helps out when things are busy, but he doesn't attend meetings regularly.

The vice-president of the club is Claudia Kishi. Claud is Japanese-American and drop-dead gorgeous, with long, shiny black hair and almond-shaped eyes. Claud may not do as well in school as her older sister, who's a certified genius, but she has her own talents as an artist. She's about the most creative person I know, and not just when it comes to drawing or painting. She's also creative about her appearance: for Claud, every outfit and every hairstyle is like a piece of art. As vice-president, Claud doesn't have many duties, except for answering the phone during non-meeting times. But she's taken on Snack Provision as her unofficial duty, and she puts her heart into making sure there's plenty to munch on at every meeting. (The We ♥ Kids Club members, who are natural-food lovers like me, would die on the spot if they saw how much junk food Claud can put away in a day. She should be in the Guinness Book of World Records for Most Chee-tos consumed.)

Claudia's best friend and shopping partner is Stacey McGill. Stacey is the club treasurer, a job that's tailor-made for a math whiz like her. She's an only child who grew up in New York City, and she's way more sophisticated than anyone else I know in Stoneybrook. She has stunning blue eyes and blonde hair that's usually permed into wild curls. Stacey's parents are divorced, and her dad still lives in New York. She visits him often, making sure to pop into Bloomingdale's to check out the latest fashions while she's there.

When I'm in Stoneybrook, I'm the alternate officer of the BSC. That means that I can fill in for any officer who can't make it to a meeting. While I'm here in California, my job is being covered by Shannon Kilbourne, who's usually an associate member. Shannon lives in Kristy's new neighborhood. She's one of the best students at her private school. (She's one of those kids who not only gets all A's but *also* belongs to every single club.)

Everybody I've mentioned so far, including the members of the We ♥ Kids Club, is thirteen and in the eighth grade. But there are two BSC members who are eleven and in the sixth grade: Jessi Ramsey and Mallory Pike. They're junior officers, and while they're both great sitters, they're not allowed to sit alone at night yet (unless it's for their own families). They take care of a lot of the afternoon jobs. Jessi and Mal are best friends, and they stick together like glue. Jessi is African-American, and she's a serious ballet student. She has a younger sister and a baby brother, and an aunt who lives with her family. Mal, who has reddish-brown hair, glasses, and braces, comes from a gigantic family: she has *seven* younger brothers and sisters. She wants to be a writer when she grows up.

Now, a typical BSC meeting follows a predictable pattern. Everybody has his or her usual spot to sit in, and as they settle in, Claudia passes around the snacks. Kristy calls the meetings to order at exactly five-thirty. If it's a Monday, Stacey collects dues. After that, the phone usually starts ringing, and with the help of Mary Anne's perfectly kept record book, the jobs are assigned. Kristy keeps the members focused on "club business" (most of the time, anyway), and at six o'clock sharp she declares the meeting adjourned.

We ♥ Kids Club meetings are nothing like that. My friends and I didn't have *any* regular meeting times until recently, and even now the meeting time isn't strictly enforced. For example, that afternoon I had arrived at Sunny's house at ten to five, since our meeting was supposed to start at five. I've been well-trained by Kristy, who's a total stickler for punctuality. Sunny and I hung out, gabbing about her new mountain bike, until Maggie showed up at around ten after. Jill cruised in a few minutes later, and a few minutes after *that* we decided we might as well start the meeting. Not that it made much difference. We talked about the same stuff *after* the meeting had started as we had been talking about before. Oh, there was one item of club business: Maggie told us about a new way to make guacamole she'd just learned.

Recipes aren't a part of the BSC agenda, but in the We ♥ Kids Club we believe that natural foods are the best for adults *and* kids. We're constantly collecting recipes to add to our health-food cookbook and our personal recipe files.

I looked around the room at my friends. Sunny is a strawberry blonde, with freckled rosy cheeks to match. I've known her for what seems like forever, since her house is right down the block from mine. We've always felt free to wander in and out of each other's houses, borrowing each other's clothes and swapping books of ghost stories, which we both love. Mrs. Winslow, Sunny's mom, is like a second mother to me. She's a really talented potter. Mr. and Mrs. Winslow used to be hippies. In fact, Sunny's full name is Sunshine Daydream Winslow. She'd probably kill me if she knew I was spreading *that* fact around.

We've always thought it was the neatest coincidence that her *real* name and my family nickname are the same.

Jill Henderson has blonde hair so dark it's almost brown — until you see her in the sun, when all the golden highlights shine through. She has velvety brown eyes and a sweet, serious manner. Jill lives in a little house in the hills, with her mom (who's divorced), her sister Liz, and three boxers, named Shakespeare, Smee, and Spike. They are so ugly they're almost cute, if you know what I mean. (The dogs, not the Hendersons.)

Now, Maggie Blume does not have your *average* hair. First of all, it's really short (except for the tail snaking down her back) and spiky, and second, she's always got some color streaked in, such as red or purple or green.

Maggie has the most style of any of us. Even Claud and Stacey would be impressed. Maggie knows how to combine thrift-shop threads with hip accessories and shoes to make a fashion statement that can't be missed.

If she sounds cool, she is. And get this: she's even cool about the fact that her house is, like, a major gathering place for the biggest stars in Hollywood! Her dad's in the movie business, and people such as Christian Slater are always dropping in for lunch or for a swim in the Blumes' gorgeous pool, which is surrounded by palm trees. In fact, Winona Ryder had given Maggie the guacamole recipe she told us about. Not that Maggie would show off about something like that. To her, it's just normal to be trading cooking tips with a huge star.

She'd barely finished explaining how to make the guacamole that afternoon, when the phone started ringing like crazy. Halloween was creating plenty of work for the We ♥ Kids Club: parents were asking us to do everything from helping to make costumes to taking their kids trick-or-treating on the big day. We scrambled to fill the jobs, and by the end of the meeting the record book was packed with entries. Kristy would have been proud. After all, even if the We ♥ Kids Club isn't run exactly the way *she* would run it, it's still based on her idea. And, just like most of her other ideas, this one is a huge success — both the East Coast and West Coast versions.

CHAPTER 3

"**O**oh, turn it up! Turn it up! I *love* this song!" Carol beat out the rhythm on the steering wheel while she waited for the light to change.

I reached over to crank up the volume, the light turned green, and we sailed down the road, singing along at the tops of our lungs.

What's wrong with this picture?

Nothing, as far as I'm concerned. I've learned to enjoy Carol's company. But a few months ago, I would have thought that a *lot* was wrong. I thought grown-ups should act like grown-ups. They shouldn't sing along to the radio, or if they do they should sing to Frank Sinatra or some other creaky dinosaur, not to the Batmatics, whose song "I Don't Love You Anymore" was blasting out of the speakers that day. Also, I thought grown-ups shouldn't wear sunglasses with neon-orange frames, or ripped jeans and MTV T-shirts, which is what Carol had on. I guess I also used to think grown-ups shouldn't drive little red sports cars.

But I've changed my views. Whatever Carol wants to do is fine with me. If she can be a grown-up and still be cool, I can deal with it, and even like it. I've come to accept the fact that I will soon have one of the hippest stepmothers in history.

"Hey, there's Sunny!" I said, turning to wave as we passed her. Carol punched the horn three times, and Sunny grinned and waved back. I swear, there's nothing like the feeling of riding along in a convertible, with your hair streaming behind you. I could *definitely* get used to it.

"Okay," said Carol, reaching over to turn down the radio. She had just pulled into the shopping center we had been heading for. It was late on Saturday afternoon, and we were out doing a few errands before dinner. "Now, what stores do you need to go to?"

"Mainly just Kopler's Drugs," I said. "I wanted to look for this new mousse I saw in an ad. It's supposed to make your hair really shiny."

"I could use some too," Carol said, checking herself in the rearview mirror. "Get two cans, okay?" She handed me a five-dollar bill.

"Sure," I said. "Oh! I also have to go to

Ellie's Variety. To pick up that green paint, for Jeff."

"Not just green," Carol reminded me, with a smile. She imitated Jeff's earnest directions: "*Monster* green. Like, it should look totally slimy and gross."

"Right," I said. I pretended to write on an invisible notepad. "Slimy and gross."

"Well, I'm going to Kopy Kwik," said Carol. "And maybe while they're copying my stuff I'll run over to Sam's Deli for some of those pickles your dad loves." We sat for a moment, waiting for the song to end, and then she turned off the engine. "Meet you back here in, say, ten minutes?" she asked, raising her eyebrows.

"Fine," I said, as I hopped out of the car. I headed for Kopler's Drugs and pushed the door open. Immediately, I smelled that drugstore aroma: a mixure of cologne, Band-Aids, jelly beans, and suntan lotion. I took a deep breath and smiled. I happen to love drugstores. It's so much fun to cruise the aisles, checking out new products and considering each of them. Should I get some of that new apricot cleansing mask? Or how about a new loofah? I could spend hours in a drugstore.

But that day I headed straight for the mousse-and-gel section, found the stuff I was looking for, and took two cans of it up to the register. Carol would be back at the car in ten minutes, and I didn't want to keep her waiting.

Next, I went into Ellie's Variety. I love variety stores, too. Where else can you find construction paper, alarm clocks, baby T-shirts, and coffee mugs with cute sayings on them, all in the space of a few feet?

If there actually is an Ellie, all I can say is that she must *love* Halloween. That store was decorated within an inch of its life. There were "cobwebs" draped over every shelf, and witches and skeletons dangled from the ceiling. Cardboard jack-o'-lanterns danced along the walls, and there were bouquets of plastic autumn leaves everywhere.

"Looking for something?" somebody behind me asked. I turned, and almost jumped out of my skin. Standing in front of me was a mummy, draped in ratty old bandages, shreds of which hung from her outstretched hands.

Then I noticed the "Ellie's" badge pinned to the mummy's chest, and I giggled. "Nice costume," I said.

"Thanks," said the mummy. "How can I help you?"

"I'm looking for some green poster paint," I said. "It's for a monster costume."

"Ah," she said. "Then you'll want our special 'Halloween Scene' paint."

"Perfect!" I said. "Lead me to it."

I followed the mummy to a display of paints, and poked through the colors until I found a green I thought Jeff would like. "Gross," I said.

"Isn't it?" asked the mummy, looking pleased. "Now, will you be needing some bloody fingers, or perhaps a hanging eyeball?"

"Not today," I said. "But I may be back, with my brother."

I took the paint to the register and paid for it. "So, this is for your brother," said the mummy, who had ducked behind the counter to ring up the sale. "What are *you* going to be for Halloween?"

"Oh, nothing," I said. "I'm too old for that stuff."

"Too old? *Never!* Halloween is everybody's chance to be a kid again. You should definitely dress up." She nodded earnestly.

"I'll think about it," I said, smiling.

"Drop in anytime," said the mummy. "I'll be glad to help you figure out a costume."

She handed me my change with a mummified smile. I took the paint and headed out to the car, hoping I hadn't kept Carol waiting. Luckily, she wasn't there yet, so I climbed in to wait. I settled back in my seat and picked up the mousse, to look it over. I had been thinking I'd try it as soon as I got home, but when I checked the directions, I saw that you were supposed to use it on "freshly washed, towel-dried hair." I stuck it in my backpack, figuring I'd use it the next morning, after my shower.

That's when I heard the scream.

I glanced around, trying to see where the sound had come from, but there was nobody in sight. Then there was another scream, and somebody came flying out of Speedy Jack's, the convenience store Carol had parked in front of. Somebody in a big, bright, silly-looking clown mask, with a huge red smile and shocking-pink hair.

I laughed at first, thinking that it was another clerk from Ellie's. Then I saw the door of the convenience store bang open again. A woman in a pink smock stood in the doorway, cupping her hands around her mouth. "Stop him!" she yelled. "Call the cops! We've been robbed!"

Just then the "clown," who had run across the traffic lane, stumbled and caught himself — on the fender of the car next to Carol's. I stared at his back for about five seconds while he got his balance. I couldn't have moved a muscle even if I'd wanted to; I felt paralyzed.

Then he stood up straight and headed for a black car that was parked nearby. A red nylon bag bumped against his knees as he ran. He jumped into the car, started it, and took off with a screech. The sound echoed in my ears.

It seemed as if the whole thing had happened in slow motion.

A second later, Carol arrived at the car. "What's *happening*?" she asked, looking first at my face, which must have been dead white, and then at the crowd gathering around the clerk in front of Speedy Jack's. A police car pulled up with its blue lights flashing and its siren wailing, and then another one pulled up right behind *that* one.

"A robbery," I said to Carol, in a shaky voice. "I saw the robber."

"Did he have a *gun*?" Carol asked, her eyes wide. She reached over and put her arm around my shoulder. "Oh, honey, how awful."

"A gun? I don't know," I said slowly. The idea was terrifying. "I didn't actually see the robbery. I just saw some guy running away." I gave a little shudder, and Carol hugged me closer.

Fifteen minutes later, I was in a little room at the police station, drinking water out of a paper cup and listening as a police investigator, Officer Garcia, asked me question after question. Carol was out in the lobby, calling my dad to let him know what had happened.

Officer Garcia was a small, black-haired woman with a gentle voice and a *very* serious attitude. "This perpetrator was armed," she had told me. "He showed Ms. Casey his gun and forced her to empty the cash register."

Ms. Casey was the woman who had been behind the counter at Speedy Jack's. She was being questioned in another room.

"Now, you said he was only about five-eight or five-nine," said Officer Garcia, pacing the room. "Hmmm. Short for a man. Okay, tell me again about what he was wearing," she said, sitting down again and flipping back a page in her notebook. "Black jeans, right?"

I nodded. "And a black sweat shirt. He had on a pair of those Fly-High sneakers, too." Fly-Highs are the coolest brand around these days. Not too many people have them yet, but all my friends want them. Their logo is a shooting star, and it's imprinted on the treads on the bottom.

"And the car?" asked Officer Garcia, her voice still gentle.

"A black Chevy Cavalier," I said, for what felt like the fortieth time. I had recognized the car because it was just like the one my step-father drives, only his is red. "No license plates. But it had a bumper sticker from Frank's Franks." The name made me want to giggle for some reason, even though I knew giggling wouldn't exactly be appropriate. I realized then that I might be sort of in shock.

"Okay," said Officer Garcia, flipping her notebook shut. "Enough for now. Thanks for your time. Just be sure to call me if you think of anything else." She handed me her card. Then she stopped me as I stood to leave. "Dawn," she said, "I just want to ask you one more time. Are you sure he didn't see you?" She gave me a very intense, serious look.

"I'm sure," I said. All at once, I understood what she was worried about. If he *had* seen me, he would know I was a witness. I could be in danger.

But I was positive. His back had been toward me the whole time. Hadn't it?

I walked back out into the lobby, where there was a bustle of activity. People were coming and going, phones were ringing, walkie-talkies were letting out bursts of static. I heard it all as if I were in a dream.

"Come on, honey," said Carol, coming up to me and taking my arm. "We'll be home before you know it. You can take a long hot

29

shower, and then relax and have dinner."

"Great," I said. Suddenly I remembered the mousse I'd bought. It seemed like years ago that I had done my shopping. I thought of Ellie's Variety and all the Halloween stuff, and gave a little shiver. I'd never think the same way about masks — especially *clown* masks — again.

CHAPTER 4

"You know what Jeff said?" I asked my friends. It was Sunday, the day after the robbery, and we were gathered at Sunny's house for an emergency meeting of the We ♥ Kids Club. Sunny had called the meeting as soon as she'd heard about the robbery.

"What?" asked Jill, giving me a concerned look.

"He thought the whole thing was 'totally awesome,' and he wanted to know what kind of gun it was," I said tiredly. "It took me, Dad, and Carol about half an hour to convince him that it wasn't 'awesome' at all. To him, the robbery seemed like some cop show on TV or something."

Maggie shook her head. "Does he understand now?" she asked.

"Oh, definitely," I said. "Especially since he heard Halloween might be cancelled. He's totally bummed."

"*All* the kids are," said Jill. "It's awful. Think how we would have felt back when *we* were little. Halloween is, like, the biggest holiday in the world for kids."

"I remember one time when I had the chicken pox on Halloween," mused Maggie. "I had to sit inside on the couch. My mom let me wear my ballet costume, but I wasn't allowed out of the house. I watched all the other kids come to our door for treats, and I sobbed the whole night."

"How tragic," Sunny said, stifling a giggle.

"It *was!*" cried Maggie, bopping Sunny with a pillow. "It probably scarred me for life." We all cracked up, but the laughter didn't last long. There was a serious problem to talk over: Halloween might end up being *cancelled* in Palo City.

Word about the robbery had traveled fast. Even before the story made the evening news, phones were ringing. The parents in our town have this phone tree they use for school news: one parent calls two others, and then those two each call two more, and so on and so on. Before Saturday evening was over, every parent in town knew there had been an armed robbery right in the middle of Palo City. They also knew that the gunman had escaped.

It hadn't taken long for the parents to make

some decisions. First of all, until the robber was caught, there would be a curfew in town. No kid under the age of eighteen would be allowed out after seven P.M. unless they had an adult with them. That was pretty strict, but what came next was worse. Unless the gunman was caught before Halloween, there would be no trick-or-treating allowed. At all.

All the kids were upset, and understandably so. Here it was, a week before Halloween. They'd been planning their costumes for months, and dreaming of bags stuffed with miniature Milky Ways and Skittles. And now the big event was called off.

But Halloween, or the lack of it, wasn't the only thing on our minds that day over at Sunny's. My friends, naturally, were worried about me. Plus, we were all really troubled by the thought that there could be an armed robber hiding out in our neighborhood.

"Where do you think he might be?" asked Jill, biting her thumbnail. She quit chewing her nails a while ago, but sometimes when she's nervous the habit comes back.

"He could be anywhere," Maggie answered. She was lying across Sunny's bed, hugging a stuffed crocodile (Sunny's childhood companion — his name is Captain) to her chest.

"She's right," said Sunny. She sat on the

floor, toying with her hair. "After all, once he took off that clown mask, he'd look like anybody else."

"I — I think we should try to find him," I said suddenly, surprising everybody, including myself.

"What?" asked Sunny.

"I said we should find him," I repeated, more sure of myself this time. "I mean, I know what I'm doing when it comes to detective work. If we caught him, it wouldn't be the first time I helped to solve a crime."

"Aren't you scared, though?" asked Jill, looking at me with big eyes.

"Sure," I said, shrugging. "I'd be dumb *not* to be. The guy *does* have a gun. But I know how to be careful. And anyway, wouldn't it be great if we really did catch him?" I leaned forward. "Just think! The kids could go trick-or-treating after all, and they wouldn't have to spend the rest of their lives remembering the time some crook ruined their Halloween."

Maggie was nodding fast. "You're right, Dawn," she said. "You're absolutely right!"

"I agree," said Sunny. Her eyes were sparkling. "After all, how hard can it be? You saw the guy. There are plenty of clues, right?"

"Whoa, whoa," said Jill. "Hold on. I want to know one thing before we jump into this. What do we do if we catch him? Make a citizen's arrest or something? I mean, he has a *gun*."

I didn't even have to stop to think. "Here's what we do," I said. "If we find out where the guy is, we immediately call the cops and let *them* take care of it. Okay?"

"Okay," said Jill, after a second's hesitation. "What do we do first?"

"Let me think about it," I said. "I'll figure out a plan."

"Don't take too long!" said Sunny. "We don't have much time if we want to save Halloween for the kids."

"I have another idea about that," said Maggie. "I've been thinking. What if we *don't* catch him? Shouldn't we do something else to make sure the kids have some fun on Halloween?"

"Great idea," I said. "What should we do?"

"Well, I was thinking we could throw a party for them," said Maggie. "At the elementary school. That way they can still wear their costumes, and we can give out prizes for the best ones. Plus we can have treats, and games — "

"Bobbing for apples!" cried Sunny. "I *love* it. Let's definitely plan it. My mom knows the woman who's president of the PTO. I bet she'd be happy for us to put together a party. The PTO would probably even help us fund it."

Jill grabbed a notebook from Sunny's desk. "Okay, what kinds of things should we do at the party?"

We all started talking at once. Planning the party was much more fun than sitting around worrying about a robber with a gun. I was still determined to find a way to catch the guy who had robbed Speedy Jack's, but until we could start working on that, the party was a great distraction.

"Maybe Ellie's Variety will donate some decorations," I said. "They have great stuff there."

Jill made a note.

"And how about if we set up a haunted house in one corner of the gym?" Sunny asked. "You know, where you blindfold the kids and make them feel different things — like peeled grapes, for eyeballs?"

"And cooked spaghetti, for brains!" Jill added.

"We can make a tape of spooky noises," I said. "Jeff would *love* to help with that. He does a great ghostly wail."

"Ghosts!" said Sunny. "We can read ghost stories in another corner." Her eyes were gleaming. Sunny loves ghost stories as much as I do.

"As long as they're not those really, really

scary ones you guys are always reading," said Jill, who was scribbling fast, trying to take down all our ideas.

"I have a collection of tamer ones," Sunny assured her. "The ones I used to read back in fourth and fifth grade. They'll be perfect."

"How about some other game?" asked Maggie. "Like maybe pin-the-broom-on-the-witch?" Everybody nodded, and Jill made some more notes.

"We have to have food, too," said Sunny. "Let's check our recipe files and figure out what to make."

The party was already beginning to take shape. I could have talked about it with my friends all afternoon, but I had to leave if I was going to be on time for my sitting job with Erick and Ryan DeWitt. As I headed out of Sunny's room, I head Jill say, "Toasted pumpkin seeds. Perfect!" I knew the party was going to be great.

At the DeWitts' house, I found Erick and Ryan playing kickball in the yard with a little boy I'd never met. Just as I walked up the driveway, Erick tackled Ryan, wrestled the ball away from him, and ran past me toward the house. "Touchdown!" Erick cried, as he leaped over the front walk.

"Hey!" said Ryan, picking himself up and brushing himself off. "Since when are we playing *football*?"

"Since about ten seconds ago," said Erick, grinning. "That makes the score eighteen to two. You and Timmy get the ball now."

Erick's eight, and Ryan is six. Timmy seemed to be about Erick's age, although he was smaller. "Hey, guys!" I said. "How about taking a break and introducing me to your friend?"

"Hi, Dawn," said Ryan. "This is Timmy. He lives across the street."

"He just moved in," added Erick. "He's in my class at school, too."

I nodded. "Well, it's nice to meet you, Timmy," I said. "I'm Erick and Ryan's baby-sitter. My name's Dawn."

Timmy smiled shyly. He had nice brown eyes, with a shock of straight dark hair hanging into them. Despite the smile, I noticed a certain sadness in his face.

"What are you going to be for Halloween, Timmy?" I asked.

"Don't know," he mumbled.

"There isn't going to *be* any Halloween," Erick said, frowning. "Didn't you hear?"

"Oh, I heard," I said. "But maybe things will work out so you can still have fun that night." I wasn't ready to spill the beans about the party, but I couldn't resist hinting. Erick gave me a curious look, and opened his mouth to ask a question.

Just then, Mrs. DeWitt — I mean, Cynthia — appeared at the door. "Dawn, would you come inside for a sec?" she asked. "I want to ask you a favor."

"Be right back," I told the boys. Inside, Cynthia was standing in front of the hall mirror, putting on a pair of gold, shell-shaped earrings that matched a bracelet on her right wrist. Cynthia always looks great. She's an actress who appears mainly in commercials, and usually when we sit for her it's because she's headed for an audition or a taping.

"I see you met Timmy," she said to me. We both glanced out of the window at the boys playing outside.

"He seems nice," I said. "Shy, though."

Cynthia nodded. "He's going through a tough time right now. His parents are separated, and he's living with his dad across the street. They don't have much money. In fact, they can only afford to rent that house because the owner lowered the price when he had to go away suddenly." She finished putting on her earrings and stood back from the mirror to check the full effect of her outfit.

"Anyway," she continued, "he's living with his dad right now because his mom's job doesn't pay much and she can't afford to keep him. But, unfortunately, Mr. Ford — Timmy's dad — just lost *his* job. He's been busy trying to find another, so I've been watching Timmy a lot for him."

I nodded, wondering where this was heading.

"What I wanted to ask you was whether you'd be willing to sit for Timmy along with the boys, whenever you come here," she said. "I'll pay you extra," she added, in a rush.

"Sure!" I said. "No problem." The extra money would be nice, but it didn't really matter to me. I could already tell I was going to like Timmy, and it would be no trouble to watch him along with the others. Erick and Ryan can be a real handful, but I had a feeling that Timmy's presence would calm them down. In this case, three might be *easier* than two. I saw Cynthia off, headed back out to join Erick's team for kickball, and spent the rest of the day enjoying myself. In fact, I had so much fun that I didn't think about the robber once.

CHAPTER 5

Dear Dawn,
Only a little more than a week until Halloween! All the kids in Stoneybrook are psyched. I bet the kids out there are, too.

I sat for the Stoneybrook version of the Brady Bunch the other day. Can you guess who I'm talking about? The kids got a whopper of a surprise. But somehow I'm not sure it was the

*pleasant surprise
that their parents
had hoped it would
be . . .*

I'd gotten Jessi's letter on Saturday, but I
didn't have a chance to read it until I came
home from sitting for Erick, Ryan, and Timmy.
Since Jessi had only given me the barest details, and since I knew she was talking about
some favorite Stoneybrook clients of mine, I
called her right up to hear the rest of the story.

I also told her the bad news about Halloween in my town. She couldn't believe it. "I
wish we could be out there to help you try to
catch that guy," she said. Everybody in the
BSC *loves* mysteries, and we've solved plenty
of them.

Anyway, the story Jessi told me was about
the Barretts and the DeWitts. That's the *Stoneybrook* DeWitts — no relation to the West
Coast DeWitts, as far as I know. Maybe they're
second cousins twice removed or something,
but if they are I doubt even *they* know it.

I don't know the DeWitt kids very well, but
the Barretts happen to be favorites of mine,
which is why Jessi thought I'd be interested
in the story of her sitting job with them. I sit

for them fairly often when I'm in Stoneybrook. When I first met Buddy, Suzi, and Marnie, it was pretty soon after their parents had divorced. The kids were kind of traumatized, I guess, and they were really acting out. In fact, we used to refer to them as the "Impossible Three." Back then, Mrs. Barrett was *also* going through a hard time. She couldn't seem to keep her life organized, and things were pretty chaotic for awhile.

Then, not that long ago, she met a really nice guy named — you guessed it — Mr. DeWitt. (His first name is Franklin.) He and Mrs. Barrett hit it off; in fact, they're going to get married! But they can't start planning the wedding until they find a bigger house to move into. Why? Because Mr. DeWitt has four kids of his own already.

See why Jessi mentioned the Brady Bunch?

Anyway, Jessi told me that when she arrived that day the Barrett household seemed almost as chaotic as when we first sat there. Mrs. Barrett met her at the door, holding Marnie, who's two, on her hip. "Oh, Jessi, I'm so glad you're here early, before Franklin," she said. "Can you take Marnie upstairs with Buddy and Suzi while I finish getting ready?"

Now, one thing you should know about Mrs. Barrett is that she's gorgeous. Really gorgeous. She could almost be a model, with her long, shiny chestnut hair and her perfect complexion. But that morning, Jessi said, she looked as if she'd been hit by a tornado. Her hair was uncombed, and she was still wearing her robe and slippers. "Marnie woke up with a tummy ache this morning," she explained. "She's fine now, but between caring for her and trying to get Buddy and Suzi ready for our trip I haven't even had a chance to dress myself. And Franklin will be here any minute."

Mrs. Barrett passed Marnie over to Jessi, who noticed immediately that Marnie's diaper was soaked. "Um, where are we going, anyway?" Jessi asked. All she knew was that she'd been hired to help out for the day, with some outing, since all seven kids would be along for the ride.

"It's a surprise," said Mrs. Barrett, grinning. "Franklin and I are taking the kids on a Mystery Tour."

"Well, great," said Jessi. "Sounds like fun." She knew the Barretts and DeWitts had been putting in a lot of time house-hunting lately, and she figured this trip was a reward for the kids for being so patient. So far, the families had been unable to agree on a house that suited everybody, even though they'd been looking for weeks.

Jessi headed upstairs with Marnie, changed

her, and then went looking for Buddy and Suzi. She found them in Buddy's room. He's eight, and his room is decorated in what Jessi calls "Early American Ninja Turtle." There was an open backpack on Buddy's bed, and the two of them were throwing things into it as they argued about where they might be going that day.

"I'm definitely bringing my Knicks cap," said Buddy. "I just bet they got tickets for a game."

"Game?" echoed Marnie.

"A basketball game," said Buddy. He picked up a dirty T-shirt from the floor, wadded it into a ball, and threw it into a hoop mounted on his door. "Score!" he yelled. "Two points!"

"I *hate* basketball," said Suzi, who's five. "I bet we're going to the toy store to buy furniture for my dollhouse." She added a pair of dolls to the knapsack. "I'm bringing the mommy and daddy just in case, so they can try out their new couch."

Jessi was about to tell the kids that no matter where they went she was sure they would have fun when suddenly she heard a honking sound from outside. Buddy raced to the window. "It's them!" he yelled. "And they rented a red van this time. Cool." He grabbed his backpack and raced downstairs, with Suzi on his heels. Jessi followed, carrying Marnie and

45

thinking how grateful she was that Mrs. Barrett and Franklin had rented a van. The first time the two families had gone out — with Mallory along as a sitter — they'd had to take two cars, and the day had been a disaster. A van would make the trip much easier.

Easier, maybe, but not exactly *easy*. After the hellos had been said, Jessi noticing that Franklin complimented Mrs. Barrett on her hastily pulled-together outfit, the families piled into the van. Or tried to, anyway. The loading procedure, Jessi said, did not go smoothly.

"I call the front!" yelled Franklin's oldest child, eight-year-old Lindsey.

"No way, Lindsey-pinsey!" said Buddy. "You had it last time. I get it today!"

"*Neither* of you gets it," Franklin said firmly, from his seat behind the wheel. "I will be accompanied up here by my lovely fiancée." He smiled at Mrs. Barrett, who was standing beside the van with Marnie in her arms.

"Okay, then, I call the window!" said Lindsey.

"Fine," said Buddy. "There's plenty of windows. Just so I get the one in the way back."

"No, I — " began Lindsey, but her father gave her a Look. "Oh, okay," she said. "I want to sit next to Taylor anyway." She plopped down into the middle seat, next to her six-year-old brother, and folded her arms. Buddy climbed in back and squeezed past Suzi, and then Madeleine, who's four. The two of them were already giggling as they shared loudly whispered secrets.

Meanwhile, Jessi helped Mrs. Barrett settle Marnie, whose diaper already seemed a little damp again, and Ryan, Franklin's two-year-old, into the two baby seats. Then she belted herself in and, without realizing it, heaved a big sigh. Franklin gave her a laughing glance in the rearview mirror. "The day's just starting, Jessi," he said. "Hang in there!"

"It's going to be fun," said Mrs. Barrett. She turned in her seat. "Everybody ready for the Mystery Tour?" she asked.

"Yea!" the kids shouted.

"Then let's go," she said. Franklin started the engine and then eased the van out of the driveway. He drove down the street, took a left, and headed out of Stoneybrook.

They drove for about half an hour, but Jessi told me it felt like *days*. The kids were very excited about the Mystery Tour. In fact, as Jessi put it, they were "totally hyper." Every two minutes one of them would ask "Where are we *going*?" and then another would ask "Are we almost *there*?" In answer to every question, the adults just smiled mysteriously and said, "You'll see," which drove the kids *nuts*.

Finally, they entered the town of Greenvale. "Oh, I've been here before," said Jessi. "Don't they have a Main Street that's all fixed up to look like it did two hundred years ago?"

"That's right," said Mrs. Barrett. "It's a *lovely* town."

Franklin pulled the van into a parking spot. "Everybody out!" he said. "I hope you're all hungry."

They trooped into a restaurant that was decorated in "colonial" style. "The King's Arms," Buddy said, reading the name on the menu after they'd sat down at a table.

"The King's Legs," said Taylor, giggling.

"The King's Big Toe," Lindsey said, which made *all* the kids shriek with laughter.

"All right, all right," said Franklin, trying to sound firm. Jessi said she saw a twinkle in his eyes. "Let's settle down and order."

About an hour — and three spilled glasses of milk — later, Buddy took the last bite of his "Knight-burger" and turned to his mom. "That was great," he said. "This Mystery Tour was a neat idea."

"Oh, but it's not over yet," said Mrs. Barrett. "We still haven't reached our final destination." She looked at Franklin and winked.

After lunch, the adults herded the kids next door to "Ye Olde Country Store," which had counters covered with row upon row of candy-filled glass jars. "Wow!" said Suzi, her eyes round.

"I thought we'd pick out our Halloween candy here," said Mrs. Barrett. "Also, you can each choose something for dessert."

The kids went wild sorting through the penny candy. There were licorice sticks, root-beer barrels, Mary Janes, candied fruit slices, and every other sweet thing imaginable. Finally, they brought their loot up to the cash register. Suzi turned to Franklin, who was pulling out his wallet. "This is the best surprise!" she said. "I love our Mystery Tour."

Franklin just smiled. "And it's not over yet," he said. "Everybody ready? Let's get back in the van and head for the *real* surprise."

Ten minutes later, Franklin pulled the van into the driveway of a big white house with green shutters and a wide, inviting porch that wrapped around three sides. The house sat in a huge yard full of trees that looked as if they were *begging* to be climbed, Jessi said, and through a gap in a fence she could see a built-in pool in the backyard.

The kids, following their parents' lead, piled out of the van and stared at the house. "Well?" asked Franklin.

"What do you think?" said Mrs. Barrett.

"About what?" asked Buddy.

"The house," said Mrs. Barrett. "It has a pool, six bedrooms, and a rec room in the basement."

"Not to mention a really cool treehouse in the side yard," added Mr. DeWitt. "And it's near a terrific elementary school, and in a neighborhood full of kids your age."

"It's nice, I guess," said Lindsey cautiously. "But why are we here?"

"Because the best thing about this house is that it's in Greenvale, which means we can afford it!" said Mrs. Barrett. "Franklin and I made an offer on it yesterday and if all the paperwork goes through it'll be ours!"

"Ours?" asked Buddy doubtfully. "We're going to move here?" Then Jessi said, he must have seen his mother's face cloud over a little. "Cool!" he added unconvincingly. "Is *this* the reason for the Mystery Tour?" The adults nodded, beaming.

"It's wonderful!" said Lindsey, with a smile that looked, according to Jessi, a little forced.

"I like the porch," said Taylor.

"Can my Barbie swim in the pool?" asked Suzi.

"Of course, of course," said her mother happily. "We can *all* swim in the pool. It's going to be just perfect!"

The kids smiled politely, but Jessi noticed that they didn't have much else to say. It didn't seem to matter. Mr. DeWitt and Mrs. Barrett were so thrilled and excited that they apparently didn't notice the kids' lack of enthusiasm. But Jessi did, and it worried her. As she said at the end of her letter:

Something just doesn't seem right about this house. I can't put my finger on it, but I'll bet the kids know what it is. And I really hope they let their parents in on the secret before it's too late...

CHAPTER 6

"**W**hy no, we don't carry *any* clown masks," said the clerk at Ellie's, running a hand over her *extremely* high forehead. (She was dressed as a Conehead that day.) "We carry makeup and wigs, instead. I'd be glad to demonstrate some classic clown faces for you — "

"No, that's okay," I said quickly. "My cousin really had her heart set on a certain type of mask she saw, with pink hair and a big red smile."

"Your cousin?" asked the clerk. "Didn't you say it was for your sister?" She looked at me suspiciously. "This doesn't have anything to do with that robbery over at Speedy Jack's, does it? Poor Carlene. She was scared out of her wits."

I avoided her eyes. I didn't really want to spread the word that the We ♥ Kids Club was working on the robbery case. "Um, no," I said.

"And it *is* for my cousin. We're just really close. Sometimes I call her my sister." I glanced at Sunny, whose eyebrows were raised. I don't think she's ever seen me lie before. That's because I rarely do it. Normally, I think honesty is the best policy. But now I thought my friends and I would be safer if nobody knew that we were investigating the case. After all, the criminal was still on the loose. If he heard that a bunch of kids — one of whom had *seen* him — were tracking him down . . . well, I didn't like to think about what he might do.

Sunny and I had headed straight for Ellie's Variety after school on Monday, hoping to find out where the robber's clown mask had been bought. We figured it would be the first step in our investigation. Also, we had other business at Ellie's: we wanted to ask for help with our party.

We'd already discussed the party with the clerk, whose name was Mrs. Stevens. She had said she was *sure* Ellie (there really was an Ellie!) would be glad to help. She'd promised to talk to her. Then I'd brought up the clown mask, but we weren't getting such easy answers about *that*.

The night before, as I was lying in bed trying to fall asleep, I had spent some time thinking about the robbery. I went over every detail in my mind, trying to make sure I wasn't forgetting any important clues. Then, out of the blue, I remembered something. I remembered staring at the robber's back for a few seconds as he caught his balance. And when I brought that image to mind, I realized that there was one tiny clue I hadn't mentioned to the police: on the back of that clown mask I'd seen a manufacturer's tag. And when I remembered what it looked like, it gave me the shivers.

It was black, with a white skull-and-crossbones.

I hadn't wasted any time telling Sunny and the others about my new clue. "Shouldn't you call Officer Garcia?" Jill asked, as we discussed it during lunch on Monday. We were eating our sandwiches in the school courtyard, on a bench near the bougainvillea tree. That tree is always covered with gorgeous pink blossoms, and every time I look at it I'm reminded of how *different* California is from Connecticut. Back in Connecticut, I knew, my friends would be eating their lunches in a noisy, crowded cafeteria. But here I was, eating under the bougainvillea and watching the hummingbirds that always dart around it.

"I'll call Officer Garcia after school," I said. "But she'll probably think I'm being silly."

That was when Sunny suggested that *we* try to track down where the mask had come from.

"The police probably won't have the time to do that, but I happen to have the afternoon free," she said.

So now that we were running into a dead end at Ellie's, I decided to try one more question. "This mask my sis — *cousin* — wants," I said. "I think it's made by this company, um, I don't remember their name, but their logo is a skull-and-crossbones."

"Oh!" said Mrs. Stevens, nodding so fast that her cone started to sway. "Jolly Roger! Sure. They make great stuff." In her enthusiasm for anything to do with costumes, she seemed to have forgotten about being suspicious. "There's only one place in town that carries that line, though: the Halloween Shoppe. You know, that place down the road, next to Sears? It's only open during October, but they always have the best costumes and masks."

"Great!" I said. "Thanks a lot!"

"No problem," she said. "Hey, by the way, did you think about maybe dressing up? Don't forget, I'd love to help." She tilted her cone and gave me an appraising look. "I was thinking you'd make a terrific Little Bo Peep."

"I'll let you know," I said, laughing. I imagined myself dressed up in a shepherdess outfit, with Sunny, Maggie, and Jill running behind me dressed as sheep. The idea was hilarious. As we left Ellie's, I told Sunny what I was picturing, and we giggled all the way to the Halloween Shoppe.

"Whoa! What a cool store," said Sunny, as soon as we walked in the door.

I gazed around. "It sure is," I said. The store was like a little cave. It was small and dark and kind of spooky. Every inch of wall space was covered with masks that hung eerily, their empty eyes seeming to follow us as we walked around looking at them. There was Aladdin, with Dracula right next to him. A little farther down the wall hung a Ninja Turtles mask, and near it was Snow White. I saw one clown mask, but it wasn't like the robber's at all.

A jumble of accessories lay on the counters: I saw witches' brooms, fake arms with hooks for hands, magic wands, "diamond" tiaras, gorilla feet, and a bunch of other weird items. A clothing rack held full-length costumes: the gorilla that went with the feet, a princess gown, a space suit, a vampire cape.

I picked up a bloody hand made out of rubber and shoved it up my sleeve. "Hey, Sunny," I said. She whirled around to look and I lifted the hand as if to scratch my head.

"Oh, *gross!*" she said.

"Can I help you?" I turned to see a cute guy — he looked as if he might be a senior in high school — stepping out from behind the counter.

"I, uh, well . . ." I stammered. I hadn't really thought about what I was going to say.

"We're looking for a certain clown mask," said Sunny confidently. She smiled at the boy.

He smiled back. "We only have a couple left," he said. "They've been popular this year, for some reason." He pointed out the mask I'd seen, which had blue hair and a white frown and looked as if it were cheaply made. Then he showed us another, which was hard plastic instead of soft rubber like the robber's mask.

By that time I'd figured out what to say. "Actually," I said, "we were looking for a Jolly Roger mask. Do you have any of those?"

He shook his head. "We only had a few in, and they've all been sold."

"*Really*," I said, shooting Sunny a glance. "Um, could you maybe tell us who bought them? My cousin's looking for one, and she's desperate. Maybe one of those people would sell her theirs." I seemed to be getting better at lying. It was easier every time.

"Well, I don't know their *names* or anything," said the boy hesitantly.

"Could you describe them?" asked Sunny, flashing him another of those irresistible smiles.

"Let's see," said the boy. "There was a guy, like, *my* age. He had longish brown hair and — hey, I remember!" He snapped his fingers. "He must be on the track team at Palo City High, because he was wearing one of their shirts. He left on a skateboard."

"Great," said Sunny. "Who else?"

"Um, a guy who must work at Hank's Flower Basket, down the road. At least, he drove off in one of their vans."

I nodded. "Terrific," I said. "He shouldn't be hard to find."

"And the last one went to this tall blonde woman," he went on. "I don't remember anything else about *her*, though," he said, scratching his head.

"That's okay," I said. "Thanks for all your help. Maybe my cousin can get her mask after all."

"Good luck!" he called, as the two of us ran out the door.

"I think he kind of liked you," I said to Sunny, as soon as we were outside.

"Oh, don't be silly," she said, blushing. "He was cute, though, wasn't he?"

"Cute, but a little old," I said. "Anyway, how about if we head for Hank's? That seems to be the obvious place to start."

"Cool," said Sunny.

Ten minutes later, we walked into Hank's

Flower Basket. A little bell jingled as Sunny pushed the door open. The flower store was a cheerful, bright, sweet-smelling place. There were glass cases filled with buckets of colorful flowers, and tables covered with healthy-looking houseplants. A man was standing behind a long counter, putting together a bouquet of yellow and red flowers. He smiled when he saw us. "Can I help you?" he asked.

"We're just looking," Sunny said quickly.

"Fine," said the man. "Let me know if I can help you find something." He went back to working on the bouquet.

Then I saw a little girl who was sitting on a stool by the end of the counter. She was playing with something. I took a closer look, and nudged Sunny. Sunny gasped.

The little girl was playing with a clown mask.

I walked over to her. "Hi," I said.

"Hello," she answered, grinning up at me. "See my mask?" She held it up. "Daddy bought it for me. It's for my Halloween costume."

"Nice," I said, staring at the mask. It was *exactly* like the one the robber had been wearing. I looked back at the man behind the counter. He was smiling fondly at his little girl.

"Tiffany's going to be a clown this year," he said. "Aren't you, honey?"

Sunny and I smiled at Tiffany and then looked at each other and shrugged.

A minute later we were standing on the sidewalk outside of Hank's. "Well, we can cross *him* off the list," said Sunny. "He's way too nice to be the robber. Plus, the mask is right out there in plain sight. No way would the robber leave evidence like *that* lying around."

"You're right," I said. "That just leaves the track-team guy. I mean, the tall blonde woman doesn't fit as a suspect. But the case will have to wait awhile, anyway. I have to be home for dinner, and tomorrow I have to sit for Erick and Ryan. I guess trick-or-treating is still off, at least for now."

I headed home, wondering if we were on the right track. Was there really any chance we could catch the robber before Saturday? If not, I knew, there were going to be a lot of disappointed kids in Palo City.

CHAPTER 7

"I think it's just *marvelous*," said Cynthia DeWitt. "The kids are so excited, and of course we parents are very grateful."

"Um, good," I said. I had arrived at the DeWitts' door in plenty of time for my sitting job that Tuesday afternoon, but it didn't look as if Cynthia were ready to go out. I knew she was talking to me about the Halloween party we were planning, and I knew she was happy about it, but her words weren't sinking in very well. The fact was, I was more than a little distracted by her outfit.

She was wearing this dowdy housedress with a tacky daffodil print. On her feet were clunky brown shoes that looked like something my grandmother might wear. She had on a pair of turquoise cat's-eye glasses, and she'd thrown a yellow cardigan over her shoulders. "Uh, Cynthia?" I began.

She laughed. "I know, this outfit is ridiculous, isn't it?"

I shrugged. I didn't want to insult her. After all, if that was what she wanted to wear, it was fine with me. I just couldn't help thinking that she looked a whole lot better the way she *usually* dresses.

"It's for an audition," Cynthia said, giggling. "They're looking for a matronly type, somebody who's totally out of the fashion loop. It wasn't easy for me to figure out what to wear, but this is what I came up with. What do you think?" She twirled around — not too gracefully, because of the clunky shoes.

"I think you look perfect for the part," I said, laughing. I have to confess I was a little relieved to find out there was a *reason* she looked like that.

"Thanks," she said. "Anyway, the audition should be over by six, so I won't be late. The boys are upstairs, along with Timmy. I think they're working on their Halloween costumes."

"Great," I said. "Break a leg!" I saw Cynthia out the door, and then headed up to find the boys.

The three of them were in Erick's room. Erick was wrestling with a huge, cylindrical roll of cardboard. Ryan was by the mirror, combing his hair. And Timmy was lying on the bed, looking at a comic book.

"Hi, guys," I said. "What's up?"

"Dawn!" Erick cried. "Why didn't you *tell* us about the party? It sounds so cool. Now we get to wear our costumes after all."

"I didn't want to tell you about it until it was a sure thing," I said. "But it looks like it is."

"Will there be games?" Ryan asked.

I nodded. "We'll have bobbing for apples, and pin the broom on the witch. And maybe disappearing chairs."

"What's that?" Erick asked.

"It's the Halloween version of musical chairs," I explained.

"Cool," said Ryan. "Can we decorate pumpkins, too?"

"Good idea," I said. "We can probably do that." Suddenly, I realized something. Erick and Ryan had been asking all the questions, and Timmy hadn't said a word. I knew he was shy, but I couldn't believe he wasn't interested in the party at all. What was going on with him?

"So, guys," I said, "tell me about your costumes."

Erick ran over to the cardboard cylinder, lifted it above his head, and slipped it over his body. "I'm going to be a roll of Life Savers!" he said, in a muffled voice. "I have these new green sneakers I'll wear. All I have to do is buy some paint, and I'm all set." He walked toward me and ran smack into a chair. "Whoops!"

"Great!" I said. "Uh, maybe you'll want to cut some holes for your eyes, too," I added. "How about you, Ryan?" I asked.

"I'm going to be Elvis," he said. He grabbed his comb again and swept his bangs into a pompadour. "What do you think? I'm going to wear jeans and blue suede shoes. And I might carry a toy guitar, if I can find one."

"Terrific," I said. "I love it." Then I turned to Timmy. "What are *you* going to be, Timmy?" I asked.

He muttered something, but I couldn't hear him.

"Excuse me?" I asked.

"I'm not going to the party," he said in a low voice.

"Not *going*?" I asked. Erick and Ryan looked shocked. "But why not? It's going to be fun, and you'll know most of the kids there." I thought Timmy might feel shy about the party.

"I know," he said. He glanced up at me, and my heart nearly broke when I saw how sad his eyes looked. "But I don't have a costume."

"No costume?" I said. "That's okay. There's

plenty of time left. You can still get one. "

"I don't have enough money." Timmy dug the toe of his shoe into the carpet. "Plus, my mom always helped me, and she's not around this year."

Oh, poor Timmy. I realized right away what was going on. Timmy was missing his mom, now more than ever. "I'm sure your mom wishes she could help you with your costume, Timmy," I said. "But since she can't, maybe I can."

"We'll help, too," said Erick. "Right, Ryan?"

"Sure," said Ryan. "Want to wear my costume from last year, Timmy? I was Batman."

I smiled at Ryan. "I think your old costume might be a little small," I said. "But I'm sure we can figure something else out. Now, you said you don't have enough money for a costume, right, Timmy?"

He nodded. "I only have three dollars. That won't get me anything."

"Oh, I wouldn't be too sure about that," I said. I was working on an idea. "I know a lady who could probably help you figure out how to put together a costume for only three dollars. How about if we pay her a visit?" I was thinking, of course, of Mrs. Stevens at Ellie's Variety. She seemed to love everything about Halloween. If she couldn't come up with a costume for Timmy, nobody could. "And I bet she could help Erick pick out some paints, and she might even have a guitar for you, Ryan."

I left a note for Cynthia, in case she came home early, and then the four of us headed for Ellie's.

"Why, hello again!" said Mrs. Stevens, when we walked in. This time, she was dressed as Lucille Ball from the *I Love Lucy* show. She had on a curly orange wig, bright red lipstick, and a funny but cute old-fashioned dress. "How can I help you today?" she asked.

"Well," I said, "Erick needs some paint, and Ryan is looking for a toy guitar. And Timmy," I said, putting my hand on his head, "is starting from scratch. I thought you might have some costume ideas. We don't want to spend more than three dollars, though."

"Ah, a challenge," said Mrs. Stevens, rubbing her hands. "Wonderful." She started to walk the aisles, and the four of us trailed along. "Dracula?" she murmured to herself. "Roy Rogers? Let's see . . ." She paused by the art supply area. "Well, here are the paints for you, Erick," she said. "And Ryan, you might find a toy guitar down aisle five. Timmy, why don't you come with me?"

I stayed with Ryan and Erick, while Mrs. Stevens led Timmy down another aisle. I heard her asking him, "Do you have some old pajamas at home? Green ones would be best."

"I think so," Timmy said. "Why? What am I going to be?" He sounded eager.

I couldn't hear Mrs. Stevens' answer. And a few minutes later, when we were all standing by the checkout counter, Timmy made Erick and Ryan go first. "I want my stuff to be a surprise," he said. We all stood aside as he passed his precious three dollars to Mrs. Stevens and received a bulky plastic bag in exchange. "Thanks," he told her. "Thanks a *lot*."

"My pleasure," she said. "I know you'll have a wonderful time at your party." She winked at me as I waved good-bye.

Back at the DeWitts', we went upstairs to Erick's room, except for Timmy, who ducked into the bathroom. "I'll be right out," he said. "I won't be able to show you my *whole* costume, since my green pajamas are at home, but I think you'll get the idea."

While we waited, Erick started painting his Life Saver costume. He'd bought a real roll of Life Savers for a model, and he checked the colors carefully to make sure they were in the right order.

Ryan combed his hair into a pompadour again, using some special hair goo Mrs. Stevens had found for him. Then he picked up the plastic guitar he'd bought and struck a pose in front of the mirror. "You ain't nothin' but a hound dog," he sang, in a silly low voice.

"Where did you learn *that* song?" I asked.

"My dad taught me," said Ryan. "He *loves* Elvis. That's why I thought of this costume."

Just then, Timmy burst into the room. "Greetings, Earthlings," he said. "I come in peace."

The three of us just gaped at him. Finally, I said, "You look *terrific!*" He did, too. He had these two shiny metallic antennas sticking up from his head, and his face was green, with purple dots and yellow lips. His hands were bright red.

"Mrs. Stevens helped me find the antennas, and she showed me how to do the makeup," said Timmy. "She said I would look just like a space alien she once met, back when she was my age."

I had to hand it to her. Mrs. Stevens definitely knew what she was doing when it came to making costumes. And she was great with kids.

"I bet you'll win a prize at the party," said Erick.

"Do you think so?" asked Timmy. "I — " he broke off in mid-sentence and dashed to Erick's front window. "My dad's home!" he said. "I *thought* I heard his motorcycle."

I looked out the window. Sure enough, a

motorcycle had pulled up in the driveway of the house across the street, and the man standing next to it was taking off his helmet. I realized I'd never seen a car at the Fords' house, and guessed that it must have been because they couldn't afford one. Timmy opened the window. "Hi, Dad!" he yelled. "I'll be right over." Mr. Ford waved and smiled. He looked like a nice man.

Or at least, that's what I thought at first. Then I saw something that made me wonder. As Mr. Ford headed up the driveway toward his house, he spotted a neighbor's dog digging in his backyard. "Get out of there, you dumb mutt!" he yelled, taking a few threatening steps toward the dog. He sounded really angry, a lot more angry than I thought he needed to be about a dog in his yard.

Fortunately, Timmy hadn't seen the incident, since he was busy gathering his things together. "I can't wait to tell my dad about my costume!" he said, grinning up at me. "Thanks a lot, Dawn." Then he said good-bye to Erick and Ryan, and dashed down the stairs and out the front door.

I watched through the window as he zipped across the street and joined his father on the steps of their house. Timmy might have been going through a hard time, but it was obvious that he loved his father. And he was definitely looking forward to Halloween now that he had his costume.

The thought of Halloween reminded me of the robber in the clown mask. If only my friends and I could catch him, maybe Timmy — and Erick and Ryan and *all* the kids — would be able to wear their costumes trick-or-treating, instead of just to the party. I knew *that* would keep a smile on Timmy's face.

CHAPTER 8

Dear Dawn,

You've probably been wondering about what's going on with the Barretts. Well, there's good news and bad news. The good news is that I found out why they didn't seem so happy about the wonderful new house their parents found. The bad news is that I'm not sure whether anything can be done about it....

Mallory's letter went on to explain more about what she'd discovered during her sitting job at the Barretts'. I called her the night I got the letter, to ask for more details, and she filled me in on what had happened that day.

Mal, as I've mentioned, has seven brothers and sisters, and all of them are still young enough to be completely captivated by Halloween. "They've been bouncing off the walls for over two weeks now," is how Mal put it when we talked. "It's, like, total insanity. Halloween is all they talk about: their costumes, the candy they'll get, what time they'll go out, which neighborhood to hit first. It's driving me nuts."

For that reason, Mal was glad to escape her house on Thursday and head for the Barretts', where she had an after-school job sitting for Buddy, Suzi, and Marnie. (Mrs. Barrett was going out with a friend to look at wedding dresses!)

"Hi, Mallory," said Mrs. Barrett, when Mal arrived. "The kids will be glad to see you. They're upstairs, working on their costumes, and they may need help."

Mal noticed that Mrs. Barrett wasn't her usual sparkly self. She seemed preoccupied. "Is everything okay?" Mal asked.

"Oh, everything's fine," said Mrs. Barrett (unconvincingly, Mal thought). "I'm sure you've heard that we found this lovely house to move into, which means Mr. DeWitt and I can start planning our wedding. Soon we'll be settled. It'll be wonderful."

Mal nodded. Mrs. Barrett's *words* sounded good, but the way she said them left Mal wondering what was wrong. Mrs. Barrett spoke in a toneless voice and stared at the floor as she twirled a lock of hair around her finger. "Well, have fun looking for wedding dresses," said Mal, trying to keep her own voice bright in an effort to cheer up Mrs. Barrett.

Once Mrs. Barrett had left, Mal headed upstairs to Buddy's room, where she found the three kids hard at work on their costumes. Well, Marnie wasn't exactly hard at work. But she *was* busy trying on the hat that went with her pumpkin costume. It looked like the top part of a jack-o'-lantern, the part with the stem. "Oh, how *cute*," Mal said, patting Marnie on the head. "She's going to look adorable," she said to Buddy and Suzi.

"So am I," said Suzi. "I'm going to be Princess Jasmine." She held up some pink, gauzy material to show Mal.

"Wonderful," said Mal. "What about you, Buddy?"

"I'm going to be Hamilton the Magnificent," said Buddy, brandishing a magic wand. "The best magician in the world."

Mal told me later that it took her a second to remember that Hamilton is Buddy's real name. Hamilton Jr., to be exact. He's named after his dad. "Sounds great," said Mal. "You guys should be a real hit on Halloween."

"I guess," said Buddy, unenthusiastically. "First we have to finish making our costumes, though."

"I need help with my princess headband," said Suzi.

"And I have to figure out how to paint this wand silver," said Buddy.

"Pupkin!" cried Marnie, sticking a finger through the "nose" of her pumpkin outfit.

"Okay," said Mal, wondering why the kids seemed so much less excited about Halloween than her brothers and sisters were. "How about if I help you?" She set up Buddy with the silver paint and a little brush and helped him lay out newspapers to protect the floor. Then she turned to Suzi, who was holding out a band of purple material that was supposed to go around her head.

"I want to put jewels on it," said Suzi. "How can we make them stick?"

"Let's try some of this glue," said Mal, who

had rummaged through Buddy's art supply box. "I bet it'll do the job."

The kids began to work intently on their projects, while Marnie kept herself amused by climbing into and out of her pumpkin costume. Mal was curious: something seemed wrong with the kids, just as it had with Mrs. Barrett. But she didn't want to pry, so she just worked quietly with them, hoping they'd talk about it if they needed to.

Instead, they talked about Halloweens of the past. "Remember that time we dressed up Pow to look like a donkey?" Buddy asked.

"He looked so, so funny," said Suzi. But she didn't crack a smile.

Mal raised her eyebrows. Was *that* it? Were the kids missing Pow again? Pow is a basset hound, a big galumphy guy with sad eyes and plenty of patience. He used to belong to the Barretts, but they had to give him away when they discovered that Marnie was allergic to dogs. Fortunately, Mal's own family had been the ones to give Pow a new home. The Pikes live right down the street from the Barretts, so Buddy and Suzi could visit him anytime they liked. It was an arrangement that had worked out very, very well. Or, at least that's what Mal had thought.

"Pow's going to be Underdog this year,"

she reported, hoping to get the kids to crack a smile.

Buddy just nodded. Then he continued with his reminiscing. "Remember how the Arnolds gave out Rice Krispies Treats one year?" he said. "Those were the *best*."

"What about the candy apples Mrs. Perkins used to make?" asked Suzi.

"Excellent." Buddy nodded.

Suddenly, Suzi put down her princess headband and began to sob.

"Suzi!" said Mal, alarmed. "What's the matter?" She reached over to give Suzi a hug, but Suzi just squirmed away and cried even harder.

"This year — " she said, between sobs. " — last time!"

Buddy looked upset. "It's okay, Suz," he said. "Don't cry."

"It's *not* okay," she said, sniffling now. "And you know it. We'll never trick-or-treat at the Perkinses again, and we'll never see Pow anymore, either."

"I know," said Buddy, looking as if he might start crying, too. "I wonder if they even *go* trick-or-treating in dumb old Greenvale."

Suddenly, the light dawned for Mallory. So *that's* what it was all about. The Barrett kids weren't happy about moving to Greenvale. It shouldn't have been a surprise, but somehow it was. Jessi hadn't mentioned a word about it, and she'd been with them when they saw their new house. "Suzi, Buddy," said Mal. "Are you upset about moving to Greenvale?"

"*Yes!*" said Suzi, her sobs starting up again. "I don't *want* to go to a new school. I like *my* school."

"We like our friends here, too," Buddy added quietly. "And Suzi's right. If we move we'll *never* see Pow anymore."

Mal digested this. "What about Franklin's kids?" she asked. "Do they want to move?"

"No way," said Buddy. "They like Stoneybrook, too."

Suzi sobbed quietly. Marnie looked from Suzi to Buddy, as if she were wondering what was wrong with her big sister and brother.

Mal nodded. "I see," she said. "Well, let me ask you this. Have you talked to your mom about how you feel? And have the DeWitts talked to their dad?"

Buddy shook his head miserably. "We can't do that," he said. "Mom is so happy about finding a house we can afford."

"And she loves the house," Suzi added, wiping her eyes with the back of her hand. "She thinks it's *perfect*."

"It *is* a nice house," said Buddy. "If only it was in Stoneybrook, it *would* be perfect."

Of *course* the Barrett kids would want to stay in Stoneybrook, Mal thought, where they'd lived all their lives. Then she thought back to what Jessi had told her about the day the kids had first seen the house. As far as she could remember, Mrs. Barrett and Franklin had made an offer on the house, but they hadn't finalized the purchase yet. She had a feeling the parents would want to know how their kids were feeling before they took such a big step as buying a house.

"I really think you should talk to your mom," she said gently. "She wouldn't want you guys to be unhappy in the new house. I can't promise you it will change anything, but at least you should tell her what you've told me."

"But how can we tell her?" asked Buddy.

"Well, let's talk about that," said Mal. "Maybe you can talk to her after she comes home, while I'm still here. I can help you out a little." She felt a knot in her stomach. Was she doing the right thing, poking her nose into her clients' business? She thought it over and decided she was. After all, Mrs. Barrett was very preoccupied lately, what with the wedding plans. She might not have noticed that her kids were upset, although it did seem as though something was bothering Mrs. Barrett. Maybe she *was* worried about the kids. Anyway, Mal thought, it was important that she hear what Buddy and Suzi had to say.

For the rest of the afternoon, Marnie napped while Mal helped the kids work on their Halloween costumes as they talked about their plans for approaching Mrs. Barrett. Mal asked Buddy and Suzi to make up lists of why they would rather not leave Stoneybrook. She told them to pretend she was their mom, and practice looking her in the eye while they discussed their feelings. And she told Buddy to call Lindsey DeWitt to tell her what they were doing and urge her to talk to her dad at the same time.

By the time Mrs. Barrett returned, Suzi's eyes weren't red anymore and Buddy was confident about what he had to say. The kids didn't need much help from Mal after all, but she stuck around for a few minutes just to see what would happen.

Without wasting any time, Buddy launched into his list of reasons for staying in Stoneybrook. Suzi joined in, and Mrs. Barrett listened closely. When they'd finished, Mrs. Barrett sat down and pulled them onto her lap. "Why didn't you tell me *before*?" she asked.

"We didn't want to hurt your feelings," said Suzi. "Because of how great you think the house is and everything."

"Oh, my babies," said Mrs. Barrett, hugging

them closer. Buddy looked a little embarrassed.

"I'm not a baby," he insisted.

"No, you certainly aren't," said Mrs. Barrett. "You're a big boy who knows how to share what he's feeling, and I'm proud of you." She squeezed him again. "I don't know if we can get out of buying that house," she said. "But I'm going to call Franklin right now and find out. Listening to the two of you has made me realize that *I* don't want to leave Stoneybrook, either. It's our home."

As Mal left (after huge hugs from Buddy and Suzi), Mrs. Barrett was reaching for the phone. "I don't now what's going to happen," Mal told me, when we spoke. "So far, I haven't heard a thing. But I do know this: sometimes it's best to let your feelings be known. And I think Buddy and Suzi learned *that* lesson, at least."

CHAPTER 9

"Well, we've narrowed it down to two boys," said Maggie. She plucked a hot-pink blossom from the bougainvillea and tucked it behind her ear.

My friends and I were in the school courtyard again, eating lunch and talking about the sleuthing we'd been doing. It was Wednesday: there were only a few more days until Halloween. We had to step up our detective work if we were even going to have a shot at catching the robber in time for the kids to go trick-or-treating. The day before, since Sunny and I had both had sitting jobs, Maggie and Jill had gone to Palo City High to watch track practice and try to figure out which of the team members was the one who had bought a Jolly Roger clown mask at the Halloween Shoppe. They'd spotted two who fit the clerk's description.

"I think it's the cute one," said Jill. "The one who wins all the races."

"They're both cute," said Maggie with a sigh. "Too bad they'd never look at us middle-school girls twice."

"Don't forget," I warned her. "Cute or not, one of them may be a hold-up man."

"Right," said Maggie. "Somehow it seems unlikely, but I guess we have to follow all the leads."

"I definitely want to keep working on the case," said Sunny. "Especially after being with Clover and Daffodil yesterday." Clover and Daffodil are two little girls we often sit for. They live next door to me. "They kept talking about how they wished they could go trick-or-treating. I told them about the party, and they liked the idea, but they said it just wasn't the same."

"It's not," I agreed. "So I'll go to track practice today. Anybody want to join me?"

Maggie and Jill were busy after school, but Sunny said she'd come along. The four of us agreed to meet later at Sunny's, to work some more on plans for the party.

"Just look for the two guys with long brown hair," said Jill, as we split up. "You can't miss them."

* * *

Later that afternoon, Sunny and I climbed the bleachers at the high-school track and found a spot to settle in. "This is perfect," said Sunny, taking a seat. She gazed out onto the green field. "Wow!" she murmured. "Maggie and Jill made it sound like there were only two cute boys here, but I see at least a dozen." Sunny can be just a *little* bit boy-crazy sometimes.

But you know what? She was right. "How about that guy with the black hair?" I said. "I love his ponytail."

"I like the blond one better," said Sunny. "The one who's stretching?"

"Okay, okay," I said. "Let's get serious here. We're supposed to be looking for suspects, remember?"

"Oh, right," said Sunny, tearing her gaze away from the blond guy. "So, where are the two guys with brown hair?"

"I see one," I said, pointing. "He's lined up for that race over by the soccer goal."

"Oh! The other one's there, too," said Sunny. "See him? He was behind the one you like, with the black hair."

"Okay, good," I said. "Now all we have to do is keep an eye on them and see if we can figure out anything about them."

We watched as the coach prepared the

group of boys for a practice race. "On your marks!" he cried. The boys knelt down on one knee, with their hands on the ground. "Get set!" yelled the coach. The boys tensed up and raised their heads to look at the track ahead. "Go!"

They took off running. Arms pumping, knees raised high, the boys ran around the track. Even though it was just a practice, you could tell they were working hard. You could also tell that each of them really wanted to win the race.

Back at the starting place, the coach stood waiting with his arms raised. As the boys came closer, he yelled encouragement. "Come on, Toby!" he shouted. "Work it, Sam! Get those knees up, Tom!"

Sunny and I leaned forward, watching intently. There's always something exciting about watching a race, even if it's not exactly the Olympics.

As the first boy crossed the finish line in a blur of speed, the coach dropped his arms. "All right, Toby," he said. The second boy crossed the line just moments later. "Second place again, Tom," said the coach. Then the rest of the herd of runners finished, and all of the boys walked around gasping, trying to cool down. The finish line was right in front of Sunny and me, so we had a perfect view. I could even hear the boys panting.

Then I noticed something interesting. The boy named Tom, who was one of the two boys with long brown hair, walked over to Toby, the winner. Toby was the *other* boy with brown hair. "Nice race," said Tom, slapping Toby five. "You did great, man." He seemed to mean it sincerely. Toby just nodded. He was still breathing hard.

Sunny and I exchanged looks. "Tom seems like a nice guy," I said.

She nodded. "Maybe," she answered. "Let's keep an eye on him, though. Toby, too."

And that's exactly what we did. We watched both of those boys for the rest of their track practice. They did short, fast runs and long, slower ones. They stretched and exercised. They practiced their starts. It was interesting to watch, but we didn't pick up any more clues about either of the boys or what they were like.

Then, after practice, Sunny and I followed the boys into the school — at a discreet distance — and hung around waiting while they hit the locker room to shower and change. We'd decided to tail one or both of the boys afterward, just to see where they went.

"Dawn," said Sunny, "check this out."

She was looking at a bulletin board near the door to the gym. I joined her, and she pointed to a notice pinned to the middle of the board.

"Halloween party," I read. "Come one, come all, to the track team Halloween party. Dress in your ghoulish best, have a blast, and help your neighbors."

"All proceeds to go to the Palo City Relief Fund," read Sunny. "Isn't that the group that's helping earthquake victims?"

I nodded. "And look at this," I said. "For more information contact Tom Murphy. Do you think — "

She nodded. "I bet that's the same Tom."

Just then, a group of boys burst out of the locker room, laughing and talking. Both of the brown-haired guys were with them, and one of them, the one named Tom, was carrying a skateboard under one arm.

I turned to look at Sunny, and the two of us raised our eyebrows. I knew we were remembering the clerk at the Halloween shop telling us that the boy who bought the clown mask left on a skateboard.

Then I saw Sunny's mouth drop open, and I whirled around to see what she was looking at. Tom, the one with the skateboard, had stopped in the middle of the hall to stuff some things into his backpack and zip it shut. And just before he did, I caught a glimpse of the same thing Sunny had seen: a tuft of bright pink hair. I looked at Sunny, and she looked at me. Then we nodded. Without saying a word, we'd agreed to shadow Tom, wherever he went.

Sunny and I have been friends for so long we can do that kind of thing. I wouldn't go so far as to call it ESP, but whatever it is, it's pretty cool.

We followed the group of boys out to the parking lot. Then Tom called good-bye to his friends, hopped onto his skateboard, and headed off. We had to scramble to keep up. He sailed off as if he were heading toward the neighborhood where Sunny and I live, and we trotted behind, trying to keep out of sight.

Now, Tom had seemed like a decent guy when we watched him during track practice, and seeing that sign on the bulletin board had given us a clue that he had a good heart, too. But it was almost as if he knew we needed more convincing. And by the time we lost him — just a few streets away from our block — we were *positive* he couldn't be the same guy who had robbed Speedy Jack's. In fact, he turned out to be the nicest, most polite, most civic-minded boy I've ever seen. Here's what we saw him do:

He spotted a dog wandering into the road and stopped to coax it onto the sidewalk.

He helped a little old lady across the street (really!), holding his hand up to stop traffic for her.

He hopped off his skateboard and bent down to tie a child's shoe. The mother (whose arms were full of groceries) looked like she wanted to hug him.

He gave directions to a motorist, nodding politely at all her questions.

He picked up litter from the sidewalk and threw it into a trash can.

He stopped to admire a baby in its carriage.

It was while he was cooing over the baby that Sunny gave me a disgusted look. "Are we wasting our time, or what?" she asked.

I giggled. "Somehow I find it hard to believe he could swat a fly, much less hold up a store."

When Tom finished with the baby, he straightened up, stepped back onto his skateboard, and zipped around a corner. We let him go. Sunny sighed. "He'll make some girl a fine husband one day," she said, with a straight face.

Then we cracked up.

We were still laughing about it a half hour later, when Jill and Maggie showed up at Sunny's for our party-planning session. We told them all about "Saint Tom," as we'd begun to call him.

"Well, we'll have to scratch *him* from the suspect list," said Maggie. "What do we do next?"

"I don't know," I said. "We'll have to think about our next move. But we can't do anything right now anyway, not if we want to make this party work. Let's meet tomorrow at lunch to talk about the mystery." I paused to unroll the mural I'd bought. "Meanwhile, what do you all think of this?" I asked, showing them the "pin the broom on the witch" poster I'd made the night before, with Jeff's help.

"Oh, it's great!" squealed Sunny. "I love those warts on her nose."

"Those were Jeff's idea," I said. "He wanted her to look as disgusting as possible."

"This party is going to be a blast," said Maggie. "And you know what? I had an idea last night. I think *we* should dress up, too."

"What a great idea!" said Jill. "I can't believe we didn't think of that before. Let's see," she went on, looking off into space. "What should I be? I don't think I can quite squeeze into my cat costume from third grade . . ."

For the rest of the afternoon, while we worked on making decorations, planning games, and choosing recipes for snacks, we also talked about what costumes we'd wear. By the time we finished, Sunny had decided to be Mrs. Claus, Maggie was planning a Pink

Panther outfit, and Jill was trying to figure out how to dress up as Marge Simpson. And me? I didn't have a *clue* what I would be. Somehow I just couldn't concentrate on my costume — not until I'd done everything in my power to catch the robber.

CHAPTER 10

"So? What do you think?" Sunny twirled around to give me the full effect.

I laughed and clapped my hands. "I love it," I said. "Are you wearing that to school today?" I could just imagine the looks she'd get if she walked down the halls wearing a bright red hat trimmed in white fur, plus red pants, black boots, and a red jacket so stuffed with pillows that Sunny looked as if she weighed about three hundred pounds.

"I should," said Sunny. "That would give everybody something to talk about, wouldn't it?" She turned to admire herself in the hall mirror. "But I'm not going to. I want to save this costume for our party. It's great, though, isn't it?" She twirled around again. "My dad had it in a closet. He wore it to some benefit party last year."

"It's wonderful," I said. "The kids will love it. Just think, Mrs. Claus making an appearance at their Halloween party! They can send some early messages to Santa about what they want for Christmas this year."

Sunny pulled off the hat, the pillow-stuffed jacket, the boots, and the pants. Underneath, she was dressed for school, in black leggings and a long white shirt. "Okay," she said. "I'm ready to go. We're not late, are we?"

"No, I was a little early," I said. Sunny and I walk to school together most days, and our routine is for me to stop and pick her up. She's hardly ever quite ready, so I've made a habit of showing up early. That way, I always have time to help her out with a wardrobe crisis, or join her in checking under the sofa cushions for her math homework.

Sunny grabbed her backpack, called good-bye to her mom, and followed me out the door. "Which way today?" she asked, when we had hit the sidewalk in front of her house.

Another part of our routine is that we try to vary our route to school as often as possible. I think walking the same way every day is boring. I like the challenge of figuring out new ways to get to the same place.

"First we'll go down Camino Del Rey," I said. I'd been figuring out this route from the time I woke up that morning. "We'll turn left on La Costa and then right on Durango. Then we'll circle back around and end up behind the school."

"Cool," said Sunny. "A whole new way. Let's go."

As we walked up Camino Del Rey, we began to talk about the robber. "I'm bummed," said Sunny. "We've been doing everything we can think of, but we haven't found one single new clue. And Halloween's only two days away. Do you really think there's any way we can catch this guy?"

I reminded her about some of the cases I'd worked on with my friends in Stoneybrook. "This clown is not the first bad guy I've been up against, you know," I said. "And don't forget about that case *you* helped me solve. Remember the surfer ghost?"

Sunny nodded. "How could I forget?"

Not long ago, Sunny and I were taking surfing lessons, and planning to enter a big competition. While we were hanging out on the beach, something awful happened: one of the top surfers disappeared. Everybody thought he had been murdered, especially when people started seeing a phantom surfer riding the nighttime waves. But Sunny and I were suspicious, so we did some detective work. It turned out that Thrash (that was the surfer's name) wasn't dead after all. Somebody had *tried* to kill him, because they knew he'd win the competition. And that *somebody* went right to jail, after I convinced Thrash to finger him.

P.S. Thrash did win the competition, and then he took off for Australia or some other place with big waves. I've never seen him again, but I still have this cool ring he gave me to remember him by. Sometimes I wear it around my neck on a chain.

Anyway, when I reminded Sunny about Thrash she seemed to perk up a little. "I guess we *do* have a chance," she said. "But what else can we do?"

"Let's think," I said. "What other clues do we have? Finding out who bought clown masks was no help." We walked along silently for a few minutes.

"Tell me again about what you saw that day," Sunny suggested. "Maybe we'll think of something."

"Okay." I shifted my backpack to the other shoulder. "Well, the robber was dressed in black, for one thing. He was wearing those Fly-High sneakers — "

"That's good!" said Sunny. "Not too many people have those yet. Maybe we should be on the lookout for people wearing them."

"Right," I said. "Let's see, what else?" Just then I heard somebody call my name, and I turned around to see who it was. "Hey, look!"

I said to Sunny. "There's Timmy, that boy I told you about." I waved. "What a cool way to go to school," I said admiringly.

We were passing the Fords' house, and Timmy and his dad were just about to climb onto Mr. Ford's motorcycle. Timmy wore a black helmet and a new-looking brown leather jacket, which his dad was helping him zip up. He waved back at me and grinned. Mr. Ford climbed onto the bike and started it up. Then he nodded at Timmy, who pulled down the face shield on his helmet and hopped on behind his dad. With a roar, they took off down the street. I waved again, but Timmy's arms were clutched around his dad's waist, so he didn't wave back.

"Timmy looks happy," Sunny observed. "I thought you said he was kind of a sad kid."

"He is, sometimes," I said. "He misses his mom. But I have to say his dad seems to care about him a lot. He can be gruff. Remember, I told you about his yelling at that dog? But Timmy does look awfully happy when he's around him."

"I'd look happy, too," said Sunny, "if I got to ride to school on a motorcycle. The other kids must be so jealous!"

We watched as the motorcycle disappeared into the distance. Then we started to walk and talk again.

"So, we'll watch out for Fly Highs," said Sunny. "Anything else we can do?"

"There's one other thing," I said, thinking out loud. "That black car he left in? It had a bumper sticker from Frank's Franks."

Sunny smiled. " 'Eat Frank's Franks,' " she quoted, " 'They're Frankly the Best!' "

"That's the one," I said. "I've never been there, but — "

"But we're going today!" said Sunny, snapping her fingers. "That's it! We'll stake out the joint."

"Think it's worth it?" I asked doubtfully.

"It can't hurt," said Sunny. "We'll just hang out for awhile, and watch to see who comes and goes. Deal?"

"Deal," I said, shaking on it. "Let's see if Maggie and Jill can come, too."

"Boy, I sure hope nobody's hungry!"

That was Jill. The four of us were standing in front of the counter at Frank's Franks, looking up at the orange-and-blue menu board. It listed all *kinds* of junk food: Claudia would have been in heaven. But for the members of the We ♥ Kids Club, that menu spelled Nothing To Eat.

"Chili dogs, foot-long dogs, Frank's Special dogs," read Maggie. "Ugh. Do you *know* what they put in those things?"

I nodded. "Pig ears and stuff, right?"

Sunny giggled. "And the rest of the menu isn't much better. I don't see a thing on there that isn't processed, cooked in tons of grease, or full of salt."

"We should have brought some sandwiches," said Jill wistfully.

Just then, we found ourselves at the head of the line. The blonde woman behind the counter looked us over. "What can I get you girls?" she asked. She looked about thirty-five — older than your usual counter person at a fast-food place. And she looked tired, probably because she had to deal with a restaurant full of teenagers every afternoon.

"I'll just have a soda, please," I said. "A Coke." I don't usually drink Coke, since it's so full of sugar, but it was the only thing I could think of to order. And we had to order *something* if we were going to be hanging out all afternoon.

My friends ordered sodas, too. Then, since nobody was in line behind us for the moment, I decided to ask the woman some questions. "We're looking for somebody," I said. "I wonder if you can help us."

She gave me a curious look. "Maybe," she said. "Who are you looking for?"

Good question. But not an easy one. "Well, it's a man," I said, "or a teenage boy, maybe.

And all we know about him is that he wears Fly High sneakers and drives a black Chevy. And his car has one of your bumper stickers on it."

The woman raised her eyebrows. "Not much of a description," she said. "I'm afraid I can't help you there." She pointed to a basketful of bumper stickers that looked just like the one I'd seen on the robber's car. "Are you talking about these?" she said. "Feel free to take one, if you'd like. They're on the house."

"Thanks, but we don't have a car," said Sunny. "I guess we'll just hang out for awhile and keep our eyes peeled."

We found a booth and sat sipping our sodas. Frank's is a popular place, and lots of people came and went while we sat there. We examined each of them closely. There were plenty of high school kids, and a couple of them were even wearing Fly Highs. But they didn't look suspicious. A group of construction workers came in, but they were all really big guys; way too tall to be "my" robber. There were also a few other booths like ours, full of middle-school or high-school girls.

We sipped our drinks as long as we could, but finally we had to give up our booth to a group of electric company workers with full trays.

We left the restaurant and stood on the sidewalk for a few minutes, talking about what we had — or *hadn't* — seen. "Did you notice how the woman behind the counter kept staring at us?" Sunny asked, after we'd discussed the general lack of suspects in Frank's.

I nodded. "I think it's because we stayed so long without buying any food."

"I have another theory," Sunny said mysteriously.

"What?" I asked. We all leaned closer.

"I think she's a cop. Undercover." She nodded knowingly. "She's staking out the place, just like we were."

"Whoa!" we all said, sure that Sunny was right. As we walked away from Frank's, I took one last look over my shoulder. If she *was* a police officer, I sure hoped she had better luck than we did. As far as I could tell, we didn't have a single clue left to check out. Our investigation was at a dead end.

CHAPTER 11

Dear Dawn,

I love a happy ending, and I know you do too, so you'll be glad to hear that everything worked out just fine for the Barretts and the DeWitts For a while there, it was touch-and-go: I was almost expecting to hear that the wedding had been called off! After all, if they couldn't find a house, they couldn't get married. But wedding bells will be ringing, and it looks like Stoneybrook's Brady Bunch will be living happily ever after...

Stacey's letter was just the boost I needed. It didn't give me any new ideas about how to solve our mystery, but it cheered me right up. If anybody deserved a happy ending, it was the Barrett kids.

Stacey's letter explained what had happened, but I had to call her anyway, just to tell her how happy her news had made me. While we talked, she filled me in on the details of her day with the Barretts and DeWitts.

I also talked to her about the mystery. She didn't have any suggestions to offer, though. "Know what, Dawn?" she asked. "I think the best thing for you to do at this point is put all your energy into planning that party your club is throwing. If it's a great party, the kids will have so much fun they won't even *miss* trick-or-treating."

I wasn't so sure, but I decided to follow her advice. I knew I'd also be keeping my eyes and ears open. I just couldn't give up my hope that the robber might still be caught.

Anyway, about the Barretts and DeWitts:

Stacey told me she had no idea what to expect when she took a Saturday job with the two families. As far as she knew, Mr. DeWitt and Mrs. Barrett might still be planning to buy the house in Greenvale. After all, if it was the only house they could afford that met all their needs, it would be hard to give it up, whether or not the kids were happy about the decision. Still, Stacey was hoping, as she walked to the front door, that the day wouldn't involve a trip to Greenvale to take another look at the house none of the kids wanted to live in. She crossed her fingers as she rang the doorbell.

Mrs. Barrett, looking gorgeous in a plain blue dress, let her in. "Welcome, Stacey," she said, with a smile. "You're just in time for our announcement." She led Stacey into the living room, where the seven kids plus Franklin sat silently.

Stacey was amazed. "It was a weird sight," she told me. "All those kids sitting together in one room, and nobody giggling or crying or pinching anybody else. It was, like, a historic event: probably the first *and* the last time they will sit so quietly in one place."

Stacey took a seat next to Buddy, who gave her a tight smile. "What's up?" she whispered to him.

"They said they had an announcement to make," he whispered back. "We figure they're going to tell us that we have to move to Greenvale, whether we like it or not."

"*Not!*" hissed Lindsey, who was sitting beside Buddy with her arms folded across her chest.

Buddy nodded sadly. "*Not* is right," he murmured.

Stacey glanced at Suzi, who looked as if she'd been crying a bit. Taylor and Madeleine sat on either side of her, wearing matching pouts.

Marnie and Ryan were way too young to understand what was going on, but they could sense the tension in the air. They sat quietly, too, Stacey said, as if they knew this wasn't the time to make a fuss.

After a minute, Stacey saw Mr. DeWitt and Mrs. Barrett exchange a look. Then Franklin stood up and paced around the room for a moment, coming to a stop in front of the fireplace. He faced the roomful of children with his hands behind his back. "Well," he said, "as we told you, we have an announcement to make, and I guess the time has come." He paused for a second. "We've reached a decision about the Greenvale house."

Stacey looked at Buddy. He was wincing, preparing for bad news.

"We've decided not to buy it," Franklin went on. Stacey, who was still watching Buddy, saw his jaw drop. She also heard gasps from some of the other kids.

Mrs. Barrett stood up next to Mr. DeWitt. "We want you to know that your opinions count in big decisions like this. And if staying in Stoneybrook is so important to you, that's exactly what we'll do."

Buddy finally found his voice. "Yea!" he shouted.

The other kids joined in the cheering. Mr. DeWitt and Mrs. Barrett just stood there grinning. Then, when the cheering died down, Franklin lost his smile. "The bad news," he said, "is that it won't be easy to find a place big enough for nine people. Not one we can afford, anyway."

"We'll all help!" said Buddy.

"Yeah!" agreed Lindsey. "We *want* to help."

"Great," said Franklin. "You can start today. We have a list of houses to look at."

Mrs. Barrett held up a clipboard. "They're *all* in Stoneybrook," she said.

More cheers.

"And the van's waiting outside," said Franklin. "So let's hit the road."

Stacey described that day to me as a "marathon." "We drove to places in Stoneybrook I'd never even seen before," she said. They saw really ugly houses, and houses that were falling down, and houses that weren't even big enough for two people to live in. Finally, Franklin pulled the van up in front of one near SMS. OPEN HOUSE TODAY said a sign out in front.

"This is pretty," said Mrs. Barrett, gazing at the house. It was yellow, with green shutters. "And it looks big."

The kids jumped out of the van and began eyeing the house. "It has a nice porch," said Buddy.

"I like the little tower with all the windows," said Lindsey. "Can that be my room?"

"Hold on, there," said Franklin. "No need to argue over rooms until we find out more about this place." He led the kids inside the house, and they scattered, running up and down the halls, checking out the kitchen, and racing up the stairs to see the bedrooms. Stacey scurried around trying to keep the kids together. A realtor dressed in a neat red blazer stood in the living room. She shot dirty looks at the kids as they ran past her, but Stacey ignored her. She had her hands full.

Mr. DeWitt and Mrs. Barrett paused to talk to the realtor about the price of the house, while Stacey rounded up the kids. By the time she had them all together, Franklin was ready to leave. His face, Stacey noticed, was looking very white.

"But Dad," said Lindsey, "I *like* this place. It's perfect for us!"

"That may be," said her father, herding her and the other kids out the door. "But it's way, *way* out of our price range."

Once they were out of the house, Mrs. Barrett turned back to take one last look. "It's such a pity, Franklin," Stacey heard her say to Mr. DeWitt. "It really is a lovely place."

"It sure is," said Franklin, "but we just can't afford it, and that's that."

Guess what happened at the next three houses they drove to? Pretty much the same thing. Each of the houses looked good at first (although Franklin *did* have some questions about the roof of the second one). But as soon as the kids started to fall in love with the house, they'd find out that it cost too much.

By midafternoon, Mr. DeWitt and Mrs. Barrett were looking extremely discouraged. "This is pathetic," said Mrs. Barrett, cradling her head in her hands. "At this rate, we'll *never* find a house — and we'll never be able to get married."

Franklin tried to comfort her, but Stacey could see that he was feeling dejected, too.

"Come on, Mom," said Buddy. "We can do it!"

"Yeah, let's keep looking," said Lindsey. "There *has* to be a house out there for us!" Stacey was glad to see that the kids were still hopeful.

Just then, Marnie piped up from the back seat. "House!" she said.

"That's right," said her mother wearily. "House."

"House!" Marnie said, more vehemently.

Stacey saw that Marnie was staring out the window. The van was stopped at an intersection near the elementary school, and sure enough, when Stacey checked to see what Marnie was looking at, there was a house with a FOR SALE sign in front.

"Hey, look!" said Buddy. He'd noticed the sign, too. "That house is for sale. And it's a nice one."

His mother turned to look. "It's not on our list," she said doubtfully.

"Can't we just look at it?" begged Lindsey. "It's right near the school. And it has a nice little front yard."

"A *very* little front yard," said Franklin. "But you're right, it is nice. I guess it wouldn't hurt to get out and take a look." He parked the van and everybody piled out.

First, they walked around outside. "There's no porch," said Mrs. Barrett.

"That doesn't matter," said Suzi. "Who needs a dumb old porch?"

Stacey could already see that the kids liked this house a *lot*.

And when the families went inside, the kids fell in love. "This is *great*!" said Buddy, when the owner showed them a basement bedroom.

"But there are only four bedrooms," said Mrs. Barrett.

"No problem," said Buddy. "I can double up with Taylor."

"And Suzi and Madeleine and I can share a room," added Lindsey.

Mr. DeWitt and Mrs. Barrett exchanged a glance. "That yard really is awfully small," said Franklin, looking out a window.

"Who cares?" asked Buddy. "We can play over at the school playground."

"Play!" yelled Ryan and Marnie. "Swings!" added Marnie.

Mr. DeWitt and Mrs. Barrett stepped onto the front steps with the owner of the house while Stacey and the kids roamed around inside, looking over the living room (bright and cheery), the kitchen (ditto), and the backyard (smaller than the front, but it had a patio).

After a few minutes, Franklin called the kids together. "You all really like this house?" he asked.

"Definitely," said Buddy.

"We *love* it," said Lindsey.

"Well, the price is right," said Franklin. "We may have found our new home."

"Yea!" yelled the kids.

"Or maybe we should say *you* found our new home," said Mrs. Barrett, gazing at the kids. "I have a feeling we'll be very happy here."

Stacey told me she felt like crying at that point, but she held it in. I practically felt like crying myself, when she had finished her story. Why *is* it that happy endings make people want to cry?

CHAPTER 12

"I know! How about somebody from history, like, um, Marie Antoinette or Martha Washington?" Jill looked at me hopefully as she pulled a roll of orange crepe paper out of a grocery bag.

It was Friday, the day before Halloween. And since the clown robber hadn't been caught yet — by us or by the police — my friends and I were moving along with our party plans. We had met at the elementary school gym as soon as school was out, and each of us was hauling a load of party decorations and favors. Some of the PTO members had offered to help us decorate the gym, but we'd decided it would be more fun to do it ourselves. We had the radio on, cranked high. The local station was playing all kinds of Halloween-related music, such as "Monster Mash." We bopped around to the music as we worked to set up the gym for the party.

My friends seemed to be worried about the fact that I hadn't figured out a costume yet. They kept coming up with suggestions, but so far none of them seemed right to me. "Martha *Washington*?" I said now, to Jill. "Get out of here! Anyway, it's too complicated. Where would I find the old-fashioned clothes?"

"Okay then," said Maggie, who was laying out orange tablecloths (printed with black witches and cats) on each of the ten tables we had set up. "How about a cavewoman? You know, with, like, a leopard-skin dress?"

"Yeah!" said Sunny. "And your hair up on top of your head with a bone through it, like Pebbles!"

I shrugged. "I don't know," I said. "I'd feel silly."

"Feeling silly is part of what Halloween's all about," said Jill. "It's the one day of the year when everybody gets to act like a little kid again, no matter how old they are."

"That's what I love about it," said Sunny. "I've always had the best time on Halloween." She bent to check on the bag of apples we'd brought for our bobbing-for-apples game.

"I just hope the kids have a good time *this* year," I said. "I feel so bad about their not being able to trick-or-treat."

"I heard that some of the parents feel really bad about it, too," said Maggie. "In fact, Mrs.

Johnson told me that a few parents are considering lifting the curfew just for that night and letting the kids go out after all."

"You're *kidding*!" said Maggie, dropping her end of the crepe paper she was helping Sunny stretch across the room. "That's terrible! I mean, first of all, what about the robber? And what about our party? We've done all this planning and everything." She looked around the room at the decorations.

"It's okay," I said. "I mean, I agree with you that it doesn't seem safe for the kids to go out. But it's their parents' decision. And if they *do* go out, we can still have our party. We'll just have it a little later."

"Sure, that'll work fine," said Sunny. "Anyway, I know the kids are looking forward to the party. We couldn't cancel it now, no matter what."

I sighed. I had come to the gym prepared to concentrate on setting up the party. I had resolved to follow Stacey's advice, and forget about the robber for the time being. But it wasn't easy.

I shook my head to clear away thoughts of the mystery, and set to work on making the haunted house in one corner of the gym.

First, Sunny and I put up some partitions we'd gotten from the custodian. Then we set out tables covered with cheesecloth, which would feel like moss to kids with blindfolds on (we hoped). We hung stockings from a rope strung across the partitions — they would feel like spiderwebs. After that, we put out a bowl of cooked spaghetti (Carol told me this stuff called *perciatelli* works best), which was supposed to feel like cold, slimy worms. We put peeled grapes in another bowl (eyeballs, of course), and a pile of chicken bones (ew!) on a plate, for witches' fingers.

"This'll be great," said Sunny, surveying the area. "Did you bring the tape?"

I nodded. "Jeff and I put the finishing touches on it last night," I said. "Carol had some great ideas, too." I got the radio/tape player. When I unplugged it, Maggie and Jill protested.

"We were *listening* to that," said Jill.

"I'll bring it back in a second," I said. "Sunny and I just want to check out the haunted-house tape I made."

"Cool," said Maggie. "Can we come see what you guys did?"

"Make them wait!" yelled Sunny, from inside the partitions. "You can come in a minute, but you'll have to wear blindfolds. We want to test this out!"

"Okay," said Jill. "But if we test out *your* project, you'll have to test out ours."

She and Maggie had been setting up the

disappearing chairs game, and also the pin-the-broom-on-the-witch poster.

"Deal," I said. "We'll be ready in a second." I brought the tape player over to the partitioned area and plugged it in. Then I stuck in the tape Jeff and I had made, and pushed "play." I kept the volume down low so Maggie and Jill wouldn't hear it until we were ready for them.

As the tape rolled, eerie noises started to come out of the speakers. There were clanging noises (Jeff, banging on a pot with a spoon), shrieks (Carol had borrowed a friend's violin), and ghostly moans (me, summoning up all the scariest ghost stories I've ever read).

"Whoa, that sounds so weird!" said Sunny. "It's giving me the chills."

"I know," I said, grinning. "Carol showed us how to slow down some of the sound effects for an even creepier sound."

"It's terrific. If I played this in my room while I was reading ghost stories, I think I'd jump out of my skin."

I turned off the tape and took a glance around. "Do you think the house is ready?" I asked.

Sunny nodded. "Looks like it," she said. "Shall we try it out on our first victims?"

"Definitely. We need a dress rehearsal for tomorrow night."

We called Jill and Maggie over and made them put on blindfolds before they entered the partitioned area. Then Sunny ducked inside and turned on the tape while I began a speech we'd written. "Welcome," I said in my ghastliest, ghostliest voice. "Welcome to the house of horrors! Please enter our haunted house, and enjoy the nasty surprises we have in store for you."

Jill and Maggie giggled. "I hope it's not *too* scary," Jill said. "We don't want to freak the little kids out."

"We'll tone it down for the youngest ones," I said, in my normal voice. Then I switched back to the scary one. *"Enter!"* I commanded, "and prepare to be horrified."

I led them inside the partition. The tape was playing softly, and the moans seemed to surround us. "Ooh," said Maggie. "Sounds like a ghost with a bellyache." She and Jill giggled again.

"You dare to laugh?" I asked, in my scary voice. "You won't be laughing after you feel these worms we dug from the graveyard!" I took their hands and plunged them into the bowl of spaghetti.

Ew!" shrieked Jill.

"Gross!" yelled Maggie. "Ew! It really feels like worms."

Sunny and I grinned at each other. Then

Sunny said, in a high witch's cackle, "How about these finger bones?" She pushed their hands into the pile of chicken bones. "I use them in *all* my recipes," she said with glee.

Jill and Maggie jumped back, right into the hanging "webs." "Ugh!" said Jill. "What's dangling all over me?"

"Spiderwebs," I answered happily. "Now for the eyeballs." I stuck their fingers into the bowl of peeled grapes.

"Aaah!" yelled Maggie. "That's it! I've had enough!" She ripped off her blindfold. "You guys did a really, really good job," she said. "The kids are going to *love* this."

"I know," I said. "They love gross stuff. The grosser the better, as Jeff always says."

"Well, our pin-the-broom game isn't *gross*," said Jill, "but I think the younger kids will like it. Want to try it out?"

"Sure," I said.

Sunny turned off the tape player and we headed over to the wall where they'd hung the poster. "You go first, Dawn," she said. "I want to scope this out. I bet I can stick the broom in the right place on my first turn."

"Oh, yeah?" I said. "We'll see about that." Maggie made me put on a blindfold, and then she and Jill spun me around three or four times, until I felt as if I might barf. I was pretty dizzy, and it took me a second to regain my balance. Then, holding the "broom" (a cardboard cutout) in front of me, I marched straight toward the poster. Or so I thought.

I heard gales of laughter behind me. "Other way, Dawn," Jill finally said, choking the words out. I lifted my blindfold and peeked. Sure enough, I was headed for the refreshment table across the room. I pulled the blindfold back down, got my bearings, and headed to the poster. This time I hit it right. I stuck the broom where I thought it should go.

More laughter.

I pulled off the blindfold and looked. The broom was coming out of the witch's warty nose. "Okay, Sunny," I said, joining the laughter. "Let's see if you can do better."

"No problem. This is a piece of cake." She put on her blindfold, submitted to her spins, and promptly walked across the room the same way *I* had. We cracked up, and Sunny peeked out of her blindfold. "Hmmm," she said. "This is harder than I thought." Fixing the blindfold, she tried again — and this time she hit the poster. But *her* broom was floating above the witch, in the night sky Jeff and I had painted.

"Piece of cake, huh?" I asked her, grinning.

She laughed. "I bet the kids will be better at it than *we* were."

"Can we try out the disappearing chairs

game now?" asked Jill. "I want to make sure we set it up right." She ran to get the radio/ tape player and placed it near the row of chairs. "Okay, everybody," she said. "You know how it goes. I'll turn on the radio, and you march. Then, when I turn it off, you each grab a chair. There are only enough for two of you. Then I'll take one chair away to make it harder. That's the disappearing chair part. Whoever gets the last chair wins."

"All set," we said, standing at the ready.

"Okay," she said. "Here goes!" She snapped on the radio. An announcer was talking loudly and quickly. "Darn," she said. "No music. Hold on while I find another station."

"Wait!" said Sunny. "Did you hear what he said?" She had turned white. "There was another robbery. Turn it up!"

Jill turned up the volume, and we all clustered around the radio. Sure enough, the "clown robber" had struck again, and *this* time, somebody had been hurt. A clerk at a hardware store had fallen while she tried to move out of his way, and she was in the hospital. The robber had escaped.

"Bad news," said Maggie, shaking her head.

"Very bad news," I said. "That's *awful*."

"Trick-or-treating will *definitely* be called off now," said Sunny.

Jill nodded. "Which means our party is definitely *on*. Good thing we're ready."

We surveyed the room solemnly. I felt terrible that the robber was still on the loose, but as I looked over our work I felt good about one thing. That clown wouldn't be able to ruin Halloween for the kids, after all.

CHAPTER 13

I woke up early on Halloween morning and lay in bed, thinking about costumes. I wanted something that would be easy and fun. Something that would reflect my personality.

Something I could throw together fast.

There wasn't much time left. I had a sitting job with Erick and Ryan that morning, and later in the day I'd be busy with last-minute preparations for the party. I still had to whip up a batch of pumpkin granola nut cookies, for one thing.

I looked around my room, hoping for inspiration. My favorite pair of overalls hung on a hook near my closet: should I be a farmer? What about the sheets that were pulled up to my chin? Would they make a good ghost outfit? I glanced at a flowered skirt I'd tossed over a chair: if all else failed, I could put together a gypsy costume.

None of those ideas thrilled me. But I didn't

have time to worry about it then, not if I was going to be on time for my job with Erick and Ryan. I jumped out of bed, dressed quickly, and headed downstairs for breakfast with Dad and Jeff.

"Morning, Sunshine," said my dad, smiling at me over his newspaper.

"Morning, Sunburn," said Jeff. "Get it? You give me a pain, just like sunburn." He grinned.

I bopped him on the head. Living with Jeff means being called names on a regular basis, but I don't mind it. In fact, I miss it when I'm *not* around him. Brother-sister relationships are funny that way.

"Ready for Halloween?" I asked. "I see you're already wearing that ugly mask."

Jeff, who wasn't wearing a mask at all, just laughed and went back to eating his cereal.

"I can't believe they still haven't caught that robber," said my dad, shaking his head as he put down the paper. "You two be careful out there, okay? Keep your eyes open when you're in stores."

"Speaking of stores," said Jeff. "Did you get the Halloween goodies yet, just in case there's trick-or-treating after all?" He always likes to be sure that we're going to give out something good, so he won't be embarrassed in front of his friends. One year, my mom actually handed out raisins and apples! Jeff was mortified. He convinced my health-nut family to give up their principles for one day a year, and since then we've always handed out the "good stuff."

"Carol's picking it up," said my dad. "I think she said she's buying carrots." He gave Jeff a teasing glance.

Jeff glared at him. "You better be kidding," he said.

"I am. She's getting some gooey chocolate stuff, I think."

"That's more like it," said Jeff.

"I'd go for the carrots, myself," I said, finishing the last bite of the oatmeal-raisin toast I'd made myself. "Anyway, I have to run. See you guys later." I grabbed my backpack, gave my dad a quick hug and Jeff a high-five, and headed out the door.

As I walked to Erick and Ryan's, I thought about what a pity it was that we hadn't been able to catch the robber. I could tell that Jeff was still hoping against hope that he'd be allowed to trick-or-treat, and most of the other kids probably felt the same way.

I saw the Fords' house up ahead and thought about Timmy. Being able to trick-or-treat would mean a lot to him, too. He was excited about the costume Mrs. Stevens had helped him with, and he'd even added a few details to it. He was going to be a very convincing alien.

As I approached the Fords', I noticed that the backyard gate in their chain-link fence was swinging open, so I stopped to close it. I remembered how angry Mr. Ford had been about that dog digging in their yard. As I latched the gate, I happened to look down, and what I saw made me raise my eyebrows. There was a dirt path leading up to the gate, and in the dirt were footprints.

Footprints with the clear outline of shooting stars.

Somebody wearing Fly Highs had been walking around in Timmy's yard. I leaned over to take a better look. There were a lot of footprints, going into and out of the yard. Then I shrugged. So what if there were footprints? It wasn't really much of a clue. After all, those sneakers were available in lots of stores. The robber wasn't the only one who had them. And even if it *were* some kind of clue, it was too late for me to follow it up in time for the kids to trick-or-treat. I decided to tell Officer Garcia about it on Monday, just in case she wanted to stake out the area.

I headed back to the sidewalk, feeling a little down. My friends and I had done our best, but we hadn't even come *close* to solving the crime. Thinking of Officer Garcia made me wonder if the police were doing any better. Did they have any leads? Or were they stumped, just like us?

As I passed the Fords' garage, something made me glance toward it. The garage door was open, for the first time I could remember. Mr. Ford usually just left his motorcycle in the driveway, but this time it was parked inside. And seeing what was parked next to it made me stop in my tracks. I put my hand over my mouth and just stood there staring.

It was a Chevy. A black Chevy. With a bumper sticker from — you guessed it — Frank's Franks.

"I don't believe it," I said out loud. Then I thought of Timmy. "I don't *want* to believe it," I said, more quietly. There was no mistaking that car. It was, without a doubt, the car I'd seen the robber jump into. That meant that the robber was —

"Mr. Ford!" I said, in a whisper. "Timmy's dad. Oh, no!"

Then I realized something. If the motorcycle *and* the car were both in the garage, that meant Mr. Ford must be home. Had he seen me looking into his garage? If so, he might think that *I* knew he was the robber. I looked around quickly, hoping I hadn't been seen. And as I glanced toward the Fords' house, I thought I saw a curtain moving in one of the upstairs windows.

My heart stopped. At least, it *felt* as if it did.

For a second I felt paralyzed, as if my feet had grown roots. Then, somehow, I made myself move. I ran over to Erick and Ryan's house, banged on the door, and waited for what felt like hours.

Finally, Cynthia pulled the door open. "Howdy, Dawn!" she said cheerfully. "Happy Halloween!" Then she took a closer look at me. "What on earth — " she began.

"I need to talk to you," I said. "Alone."

She nodded. She seemed to understand that I had something very serious to tell her. "The boys are upstairs," she said, "putting the finishing touches on their costumes. Come on into the kitchen." She walked quickly, and I followed her, my head buzzing with thoughts. She handed me a glass of water and sat me down at the table. Then, after she'd made a quick phone call to cancel her plans, she sat down across from me.

I took a sip of water and felt its chill slip all the way down to my stomach. Then I drew a deep breath and let it out slowly.

"What is it, Dawn?" Cynthia asked, leaning over to take my hand. "Tell me."

"Mr. Ford," I said, my voice squeaking a little.

"Mr. Ford?" Cynthia looked confused.

"He's the one who robbed that store," I said, all in a hurry so the words ran together. "In a clown mask. It was him."

"Dawn!" said Cynthia. "Are you sure? How do you know?"

"I'm as sure as I can be." I felt a little calmer now that we were talking about it. "I saw the getaway car parked in his garage. And there are Fly High footprints in his backyard."

"Oh, my," said Cynthia, leaning back in her chair. "Oh, my."

"What do we *do*?" I asked. I was feeling a little panicky. After all, Mr. Ford had been carrying a *gun* that day in the parking lot.

"Do?" she said. "Well, I guess we call the police. Thank goodness Timmy is away for the morning. He's visiting his cousin." She passed a hand over her forehead. "This is just awful," she said, sounding a little dazed.

"I know. I still can't believe it. But what other explanation can there be?" I stood up, went to the phone, and dialed. "Officer Garcia, please," I said.

A police car pulled up across the street just a few minutes after I'd made my call. I didn't watch as they took Mr. Ford away. I couldn't stand to think of Timmy's beloved dad in handcuffs.

A few minutes after *that*, another police car pulled up in front of the DeWitts' house, and an officer climbed out and came up the walk. He was looking for me. Cynthia showed us both into the den, and for the next fifteen minutes I gave the officer, whose name was Sergeant Sweetzer, a statement about what I'd seen.

Later, as Cynthia and I were saying goodbye to Sergeant Sweetzer, Erick and Ryan came flying down the stairs. "Wow!" said Erick, stopping in his tracks when he saw a police officer standing in his front hall. "Are you a *real* cop, or is that a Halloween costume?"

Sergeant Sweetzer smiled. "I'm a real cop," he said. He tipped his hat and let himself out.

"What was *he* doing here?" Erick asked.

Cynthia and I exchanged a quick glance. "He was — he was here to tell us that the robber has been caught," said Cynthia. "Isn't that wonderful?"

I gave her a little smile. There was no reason — yet — to tell the boys that their friend's dad was a criminal. Poor Timmy was going to have to deal with that soon enough.

"They caught him?" asked Ryan. "Really?"

"Awesome!" yelled Erick. "That means we can go trick-or-treating, right?"

"Well — " Cynthia began. "I don't — "

"Oh, please, mom?" begged Ryan.

"You said we could go if they caught him," Erick reminded her.

"I did, didn't I?" She looked questioningly at me, and I shrugged, as if to say 'why not?'. "Well, I suppose it would be all right," she said.

"Yea!" The boys burst into cheers.

"I'm going to go call Tommy," said Erick. "And Brad, and — and *everybody*! Wait till they hear *this*!"

And that was that. Within minutes, the news would be all over town. Trick-or-treating was on again. I would have to call my friends and let them know that our party would take place a little later than we'd planned. We would also have to make lots of calls to let clients know we could take their kids trick-or-treating after all. But I didn't mind. I'd gotten my wish — the robber had been caught. But somehow, it was hard to be *completely* happy about it. I kept thinking about how Timmy would look when he found out about his dad. I knew no amount of candy was going to make him feel any better.

CHAPTER 14

"Ooh, what have we here?"

I watched with pleasure from the sidewalk as the woman at the door smiled at my charges, complimented them on their costumes, and dropped goodies into their bags. I might not have approved of all those goodies going into the kids' bellies, but for once I wasn't going to say a thing about how bad sugar is for your teeth and body. I was just going to let the kids enjoy their day to the fullest.

I smiled as Stephie, Clover, and Daffodil came tripping back to me. I was taking the girls around for trick-or-treating, while Sunny took Erick, Ryan, and Timmy. We'd agreed to split up, so as not to overwhelm people by appearing at their doors with six kids. "Look what *we* got!" said Stephie, holding up a tiny Snickers bar. "And the lady said I was the prettiest ballerina she ever saw!"

"And I'm the most beautiful good witch," said Daffodil.

"And I'm the cutest bunny!" Clover added. "That lady sure did like our costumes."

"I like them, too," I said. "You guys look terrific." They really did, too. Stephie, who's eight, was wearing a pink tutu with spangles all over it, white tights and a white leotard, and pink ballet slippers. She had a little "diamond" tiara perched on her head. Clover, who's only six, was wearing a rabbit costume her mom had made: a gray suit (made out of dyed sleeper pajamas) with a tail, and a hat with pink bunny ears on it. She had drawn whiskers on Clover's face with an eyebrow pencil. Daffodil, who's nine, was wearing a pink, gauzy dress with puffed sleeves, and she carried a magic wand with pink and purple ribbons streaming from the gold star on top. She was supposed to be Glinda, the good witch from *The Wizard of Oz*.

"How come *you're* not wearing a costume?" Stephie asked.

"I will be, later," I said. "At the party."

"What are you going to be?" asked Daffodil, taking my hand as we walked to the next house.

"Not telling," I said. "It's a surprise!" I tried to look mysterious.

I had finally figured out a costume that afternoon. The idea had just *come* to me, and I realized it was perfect. Carol had helped me figure out how to create the costume, and I was ready to slip into it as soon as I finished taking the girls trick-or-treating. But my costume really *was* a secret. I hadn't even told my friends in the We ♥ Kids Club what I was going to be.

We'd agreed to save our costumes for the party, figuring we'd have a half hour or so to change while the kids ate a quick dinner between trick-or-treating and the party. Then we'd rush over to the school gym just in time to greet our guests.

Earlier that day, I'd been worried about how Timmy would deal with the news about his dad. But Cynthia had solved the problem, at least temporarily. "I don't think we should tell him until we *have* to," she'd said. "Let's not ruin Halloween for him."

When Timmy came back from visiting his cousins, Cynthia was waiting for him. She told him some story she'd cooked up about why his dad had to go away suddenly, and she said she'd be happy to help him put on his costume. (She'd promised the police that she'd be responsible for Timmy.) Timmy was so excited about trick-or-treating that he didn't even ask any questions. Now the little alien was out with Sunny, bagging all the goodies he could.

And I was with *my* group, watching as they walked up to each house, rang the bell, and yelled "Trick or treat!" (Or, in Daffodil's case, *whispered* it. She's a little shy sometimes.) Watching this scene stirred up happy memories of Halloween when *I* was a little kid. I'd always loved dressing up. Even then, though, I didn't like candy so much. I'd give most of my booty away to friends, or, when he was old enough, to Jeff.

It wasn't quite dark out yet, as I knew it would be in Stoneybrook at that time of day. But the sun was going down, and the shadows were growing. I started to think about some of my favorite ghost stories, just to get in the Halloween mood. I remembered one about a house where a little girl had died of influenza. Her ghost haunts the playroom, rearranging furniture in the dollhouse and "tucking in" the now-antique stuffed animals that are still kept for her to play with.

Remembering the story gave me a fun little shiver. I decided I'd tell it during our haunted storytime that night at the party. Then just as I was trying to recall some more details, I saw something that gave me a *not*-so-fun shiver. It was a figure dressed in black, flitting through the yard between two houses. I stopped to stare, but before I could see any more the figure had disappeared.

"Creepy," I muttered. Then I laughed at myself. After all, it *was* Halloween. The streets and yards were full of kids dressed as skeletons, ghosts, and witches. If I was going to get creeped out by everything I saw, it was going to be a long evening. "Come on, girls, let's keep moving!" I said to my charges, who had taken a seat on the curb in order to assess how much candy they'd raked in so far.

"Look at *this*!" said Daffodil, holding up a full-sized Hershey bar. "Those people always give the best stuff."

"I like Smarties best," said Stephie, unwrapping a roll of them.

"Hold on, Stephie," I said. "Your dad said you weren't supposed to do too much munching as you went along, remember?"

"Oh, right," she said, looking a little guilty. "Can I just have one?"

"Okay," I said. "But remember, we're going to have some treats at the party, too."

"And play games, right?" asked Daffodil.

"That's right," I said. "And no using your magic wand to help you win, either, Miss Glinda!"

Daffodil giggled.

"Let's move on," I said again. "It's getting dark, and I promised your parents you'd be home for dinner."

We proceeded down the sidewalk. The girls

walked slowly, their full treat bags bumping against their knees. Then, all of a sudden, Daffodil shrieked. "Aaah!" she cried. "Did you see that?"

"What is it?" I asked, alarmed. I hadn't seen anything.

"A black cat!" said Daffodil. "It ran right across the street in front of us, up there by Erick and Ryan's house."

"I guess that cat knows it's Halloween," I said soothingly.

"But it's bad luck!" said Stephie.

"Not tonight," I said, making up a new superstition as I went along. "On Halloween night it's *good* luck for a black cat to cross your path."

"Really?" asked Daffodil.

"Really," I said. "Cross my heart." I smiled at her, but inside I felt another of those little shivers. Then we passed a group of kids dressed as the Three Stooges: Moe, Larry, and Curly.

"Nyuk, nyuk, nyuk," said Moe, sounding just like the real thing. He pretended to stick his fingers into Curly's eyes.

I laughed out loud, forgetting about my shivers. Then I led the girls on down the street. They stopped at three more houses, and after the third I checked my watch. "It's about time to finish up, girls," I said.

"Awww, really?" asked Clover.

"Yup. You can go to the next house, but after that I'll have to take you home. You don't want to be late for the party, do you?"

Daffodil looked at the house we were standing in front of. "But there's nobody home here," she said. "The lights are all out."

I looked up. "Oh!" I said. It was the Fords' house. I hadn't realized we were approaching it. Of *course* nobody was home: Timmy was out trick-or-treating, and Mr. Ford was . . . in *jail*. "I mean, that's okay," I said quickly, trying to hide my surprise. "We'll just go to the next one."

We walked past the blank, dark windows of the Fords' house. The kids trotted ahead of me, eager to reach the next house, which was lit up brightly and had three jack-o'-lanterns on its front steps. As I walked behind them, I glanced into the Fords' backyard.

Shivers again. *Major* shivers.

Somebody was *in* that yard. I stopped walking, letting the girls run ahead, and stared into the dusky gloom, trying for a better look. Then I gasped and took two steps back. It was as if my body reacted before my mind did, and my body was saying "Run away! Run away!" Here's what my body was reacting to: the robber who held up Speedy Jack's was standing in the middle of the Fords' backyard! He was wearing the same all-black outfit (*that's* who I must have seen running through the yards) and the very same clown mask, with the silly pink hair. His back was to me, so he didn't see me looking.

I put my hand over my mouth. My brain was still working hard, trying to make sense of what I was seeing. It was so bizarre that I couldn't take it in right away. First of all, the clown was *digging* in the yard. And, if that wasn't strange enough, the clown was digging in the same spot where that dog had been digging only a few days earlier.

Of course, that still wasn't the weirdest thing. The *weirdest* thing was that if I was seeing the robber in Timmy's backyard, then Mr. Ford wasn't the robber — because at that very moment he was with the police!

"Oh, no!" I whispered. I ran to the house next door. The girls were just coming down the walk. "Clover, Daffodil, Stephie!" I said. "Come with me! Right now! I need to go over to Erick and Ryan's for a second." I tried to keep the panic out of my voice, since I didn't want to scare them. But I did want to get them off the streets as quickly as possible.

"Oh, goody," said Daffodil. "You mean we can go to one more house?"

"Sure, sure," I said, herding them across the street. Glancing over my shoulder to make sure the robber hadn't seen us, I banged on the DeWitts' door.

Cynthia threw it open. "Dawn!" she said, before I could open my mouth. "I'm so glad you're here." She smiled brightly at Clover, Daffodil, and Stephie. "Girls, I want you to go on upstairs and show Erick and Ryan and Timmy your candy, all right? Sunny is up there with them."

The kids ran upstairs eagerly. "Cynthia," I said, as soon as they were out of earshot, "the police have the wrong man!"

"I know, honey," said Cynthia. "That's why I was so happy to see you and the kids. I didn't want to say anything in front of the girls, but the police just made an announcement over the radio. They want everybody inside, off the streets."

"I saw — " I began.

Cynthia didn't seem to hear me. "Mr. Ford — John — was able to prove without a doubt that he was at a job interview at the time of the first robbery," she went on.

"That's great," I said, "but — " I wanted to get to a phone *fast* to call the police and let them know about the robber in the Fords' backyard.

"I'm so happy for John," said Cynthia. She was so keyed up she didn't seem to notice that I had something to say. "But I'm frightened, too. This means the robber is still at large."

"That's what I'm trying to tell you!" I finally burst out, not caring anymore if I sounded rude. "He's at large *right now*, across the street. I have to call the police!"

CHAPTER 15

The police arrived within minutes. Cynthia and I watched from the window as several squad cars pulled up silently — no sirens, no flashing lights — and police officers jumped out and quietly surrounded the Fords' backyard.

It happened so fast I almost missed it. The capture wasn't like the ones on TV, with chases and gunfights. I looked away for just a second, and when I looked back the cops were leading the guy in the clown mask toward one of the cars. His hands were cuffed behind him, and his head was down.

"I *have* to see who it is," I said. I opened the front door and ran outside before Cynthia could stop me. I ran right up to the small crowd of officers, with Cynthia following. We arrived just in time to see Officer Garcia reach over and pull the mask off the robber's head.

I gasped, thinking there had been a terrible

mistake. The person under the mask wasn't a man at all.

It was a woman.

The blonde woman from Frank's Franks, the one behind the counter who had stared at us that day. The one Sunny had pegged as an undercover agent. Now I was totally confused.

There was a brief silence. Officer Garcia looked at the woman's face, down at the mask in her hand, and back at the woman. Then she began to speak. For a second, I expected her to say something about having made a mistake. But instead, she said, "You're under arrest. You have the right to remain silent. . . ."

I looked at Cynthia. She was staring at the woman, frowning as if she were trying to remember something. The woman didn't meet Cynthia's gaze; she was looking down at her feet (she was wearing Fly-Highs!) and I heard her sniff. She was crying!

Just as Officer Garcia finished her speech, another officer handed her something wrapped in a plastic bag. "This was in the yard, there," he said. "Where she was digging."

Officer Garcia took the object and looked at it. Even from where I was standing, I could see that it was a gun. So *that's* why she had been digging in the yard. She must have been hiding her gun there. And the dog that was digging that day must have been hoping for a bone, instead. I stifled a terrible impulse to giggle.

Officer Garcia handed the gun back. "Tag this as evidence," she said, "along with that mask."

Then Cynthia stepped forward. "Evelyn?" she said. The woman looked up, but she didn't smile. "Evelyn *Ford*?" The woman nodded, slowly. She looked as if she were in shock.

Suddenly my stomach seemed to do a backflip. Ford? Was this woman related to Timmy somehow?

Cynthia stepped back so she was standing next to me and whispered into my ear. "That's Timmy's mother," she said.

My stomach did another backflip. "What — ? Why — ?" I began. I had so many questions I didn't even know where to start.

"Why?" Cynthia echoed my question. "Evelyn, *why*?"

"You don't have to talk, ma'am," one of the officers reminded Mrs. Ford. "Not without a lawyer present."

"A lawyer?" said Mrs. Ford softly. "No lawyer's going to be able to help me. I did it. I robbed those stores. I admit it." She paused, looking at Cynthia. "And if you want to know why," she said, a little more loudly, "I'll tell you. It was for my boy. For Timmy." She started to cry.

Officer Garcia put her arm around Mrs. Ford's shoulders. "Are you ready to come with us?" she asked gently. One of the other officers stepped forward to open the back door of a police car parked nearby.

"I'll come," said Mrs. Ford. "But first I just want to explain something." She turned pleading eyes toward Cynthia. "I love my son," she said quietly. "And I want so badly for him to live with me. But how can I support him on what I make at that — that *hot dog* place? Do you *know* what they pay? It's not enough." She paused, looked down at her shoes, and started to cry again. "I had to spend almost a whole week's paycheck just to get shoes comfortable enough for standing all day," she said. "I know it wasn't right to hold up those stores. But I just couldn't think of any other way."

"You could have asked me for help," said Cynthia, near tears herself. "I would have tried to help you figure something out."

"Thanks for saying so," Mrs. Ford said with a trembly smile. She turned to Officer Garcia. "I want to make sure my husband doesn't get into any trouble," she said. "We're separated, and he doesn't know a thing about this. I used his car when I knew he wasn't home." She closed her eyes for a moment. "He might have heard that the car used in the robberies looked like his. I think that's why he kept the garage door closed all the time."

"That's probably right," said Cynthia softly.

"He's a good dad, John is," said Mrs. Ford, speaking to Cynthia again. "Timmy will be safe and happy with him. I know that. But will you keep an eye on him, too? For me?"

"I'll be glad to," said Cynthia, wiping her eyes.

I couldn't stop staring at Mrs. Ford. She was obviously a very troubled woman, and I felt terrible for her, even though what she had done was wrong. She had done it out of love for Timmy. It was so sad.

The officer stepped forward then to help Mrs. Ford into the squad car. She sat down in the back and stared straight ahead as the car started up and drove away. The whole scene had taken only a few minutes. I stood there, stunned.

"I want to thank you, Dawn," said Officer Garcia, before she got into *her* car. "You were a big help."

"A big help?" I said. "Are you kidding? Everything I did was wrong. I was sure the robber was a man, for one thing. And I told you to arrest the wrong person. I messed up, totally."

"That's not true," she said. "You made some incorrect assumptions. We all did. A few hours ago, the evidence certainly pointed to Mr. Ford. And *none* of us thought that the robber might be a woman." She shook her head. "But you knew what to do when you saw the criminal. You called us right away, and that's the main thing." She slid behind the wheel of her car. "By the way, Mr. Ford should be home soon. We'll want to question him all over again, now — for background on his wife. He knows his son is in good hands with the two of you. Anyway, thanks again!" she called, waving as she drove off.

Cynthia and I looked at each other.

"Wow," I said.

"Wow is right," she answered. She took a deep breath and let it out. "Now, don't we have a party to go to? We'd better get moving." Cynthia had agreed to be one of the chaperones at the party. "Let's not tell Timmy anything for now," she said. "He can enjoy the party, and by the time he comes back, his dad will be home. I'm sure John will figure out the right way to explain what's happened."

We headed back inside to find that the kids hadn't missed us at all. They'd been too busy trading candy, and every one of them had chocolate smears around their mouths.

An hour later, the party was in full swing. The gym looked *awesome* with the lights turned down low and all the decorations up. There was the sound of shrieking as kids took their turns going through our haunted house, and of music blaring and then stopping suddenly as another group of kids played disappearing chairs.

There must have been fifty kids at the party, all dressed in costumes and all having a terrific time. Oh, sure, there were a few teary episodes and a couple of screaming fits, but what can you expect from a bunch of kids who have been munching on candy all day long?

"They're having a blast, aren't they?" Maggie asked me. She and I were standing near the refreshment table, taking a break with some Fruit Chewies while Sunny and Jill supervised the games. "I think Clover looks adorable!"

"She does, doesn't she?" I said, admiring Clover's bunny costume again.

Maggie adjusted the ears on her Pink Panther headpiece. "And Timmy's alien costume is great," she added.

"I agree," I said. "I have a feeling he'll win a prize."

"Speaking of which," said Maggie, nodding toward the end of the gym where we'd set up a platform. "It looks like the judges are about ready to announce the winners."

Up on the platform were Mrs. Stevens (from Ellie's Variety), dressed as the Bride of Frankenstein, and Cynthia, wearing that hilarious matron costume. Mrs. Stevens was trying to get everyone's attention. "Kids!" she called. "Kids?" She clapped her hands, but nobody heard her.

I walked up to the platform, stuck two fingers in my mouth, and gave a loud, piercing whistle. My dad taught me how to do that, and it's a talent that really comes in handy once in awhile. It certainly worked that night. Every single kid dropped what he was doing and looked up at the stage.

"Thank you!" said Mrs. Stevens. "Now, I'd like to announce the winners of the costume contest. Cynthia and I had a very, very hard time choosing, since all of your costumes are so wonderful, but I think you'll agree with me that the winner for best costume *has* to go to Timmy Ford."

A cheer went up. Everybody *loved* Timmy's alien costume. Timmy approached the stage shyly and accepted his chocolate trophy with a grin. "Grblopep," he said. "That means 'thank you' on the planet I come from!"

Everybody cracked up. Then they burst into applause. Timmy took a bow and left the platform. Cynthia and Mrs. Stevens continued to hand out dozens of prizes for everything from "cutest" (that went to Clover, naturally) to "most original" (which went to Erick, who was wearing his Life Savers outfit). A few kids I didn't know won prizes: a boy dressed as Captain Hook won "fanciest," and a girl wearing a baseball uniform won for "most athletic."

Finally, Mrs. Stevens announced that all the prizes had been given out.

Cynthia tapped her on the shoulder. "Aren't you forgetting one?" she asked. She leaned over and whispered in Mrs. Stevens' ear.

"Oh, of course!" said Mrs. Stevens. "We do have one final prize. It's for "best last-minute costume," and it goes to one of the hosts of this wonderful party. Dawn Schafer — I mean, Pippi Longstocking — will you come up here please and accept your trophy?"

I was so surprised that I jumped back, and my braids (which were sticking straight out from my head) bounced. Then I clomped up to the platform in my dad's shoes.

"Congratulations, Dawn," said Cynthia, winking at me.

"Great costume," said Mrs. Stevens.

"Thanks," I replied. "I loved being Pippi back when I was eight, and it's even more fun, now." I looked at the chocolate trophy and wondered what I'd do with it. Maybe I could send it to Stoneybrook. Claudia would *love* it! I turned and waved to the crowd of kids. "Happy, happy Halloween, everybody!" I yelled.

About the Author

ANN M. MARTIN did *a lot* of baby-sitting when she was growing up in Princeton, New Jersey. She is a former editor of books for children, and was graduated from Smith College.

Ms. Martin lives in New York City with her cats, Mouse and Rosie. She likes ice cream and *I Love Lucy*; and she hates to cook.

Ann Martin's Apple Paperbacks include *Yours Turly, Shirley*; *Ten Kids, No Pets*; *With You and Without You*; *Bummer Summer*; and all the other books in the Baby-sitters Club series.

Look for #18

STACEY AND THE MYSTERY AT THE EMPTY HOUSE

After breakfast, I realized that I'd better hurry if I wanted to finish my chores at the Johanssens' and still make it to school on time. I ran to the closet and grabbed my new coat. Then I couldn't resist modeling it for my mom. "First day for the new coat!" I said.

"It really is a lovely one," said my mom, reaching out to touch the furry trim. "You look gorgeous in it, too."

"Thanks," I said. I grabbed my shoulder bag. "See you tonight!"

I ran out the door and started to jog toward the Johanssens', but after about half a block I was already way overheated. That coat is *warm!* I slowed down to a fast walk, and arrived a few minutes later.

The Johanssens' newspaper was sitting on their front doormat. "We *could* stop delivery,"

Dr. Johanssen had said, "but we'd rather not broadcast it around that we're going to be away for so long." That had made sense to me, and I'd promised to bring it inside first thing every morning.

I stood on the front porch, rummaging through my pockets again for that key. I expected to hear Carrot start barking any minute, the way he had the day before, but there was no noise from inside.

Suddenly, I felt a little nervous.

Maybe I'd relaxed too soon about that escaped prisoner. What if — what if he had ended up at the *Johanssens'* the night before, and discovered that their empty house made a perfect hiding place? What if he was in there right now, waiting for me to walk in? What if he had done something horrible to Carrot?

Finally, I found the key. My hand shook as I put it into the keyhole and turned it. Then I pushed open the door. "Carrot?" I called. My voice came out all quavery.

There was no response.

"Carrot?" I called again, a little more loudly. I stepped to the left and peeked into the living room. No Carrot. I walked to my right and checked the dining room. Carrot was nowhere in sight.

I felt a shiver go down my spine, and pulled my coat closer around me.

THE BIGGEST BSC SWEEPSTAKES EVER!

Scholastic and Ann M. Martin want to thank all of the Baby-sitters Club fans for a cool 100 million books in print! Celebrate by sending in your entry now!

ENTER AND YOU CAN WIN:

• *10 Grand Prizes:* Win one of ten $2,500 prizes! Your cash prize is good towards any artistic, academic, or sports pursuit. Take a dance workshop, go to soccer camp, get a violin tutor, learn a foreign language! You decide and Scholastic will pay the expense up to $2,500 value. Sponsored by Scholastic Inc., the Ann M. Martin Foundation, Kid Vision, Milton Bradley® and Kenner® Products.

• *100 First Prizes:* Win one of 100 fabulous runner-up gifts selected for you by Scholastic including a limited supply of BSC videos, autographed limited editions of Ann Martin's upcoming holiday book, T-shirts, board games and other fabulous merchandise!

Just fill in the coupon below or write the information on a 3" x 5" piece of paper and mail to: **THE BSC REMEMBERS SWEEPSTAKES,** Scholastic Inc., P.O. Box 7500, 2931 East McCarty Street, Jefferson City, MO 65102. Entries must be postmarked by 10/31/94.

Send to Scholastic Inc., P.O. Box 7500, 2931 East McCarty Street, Jefferson City, MO 65102.

- -

THE BSC REMEMBERS SWEEPSTAKES

Name _____ Birthdate _____

Address _____ Phone# _____

City _____ State _____ Zip _____

Where did you buy this book? ❑ Bookstore   ❑ Other(Specify)

Name of Bookstore _____

BSCR19

ENTER SCHOLASTIC'S

THE BSC REMEMBERS
SWEEPSTAKES

Official Rules:

No purchase necessary. To enter use the official entry form or a 3" x 5" piece of paper and hand print your full name, complete address, day telephone number and birthdate. Enter as often as you wish, one entry to an envelope. Mechanically reproduced entries are void. Mail to THE BSC REMEMBERS Sweepstakes at the address provided on the previous page, postmarked by 10/31/94. Scholastic Inc. is not responsible for late, lost or postage due mail. Sweepstakes open to residents of the U.S.A. 6-15 years old upon entering. Employees of Scholastic Inc., Kid Vision, Milton Bradley Inc., Kenner Inc., Ann M. Martin Foundation, their affiliates, subsidiaries, dealers, distributors, printers, mailers, and their immediate families are ineligible. Prize winners will be randomly drawn from all eligible entries under the supervision of Smiley Promotion Inc., an independent judging organization whose decisions are final. Prizes: Ten Grand Prizes each $2,500 awarded toward any artistic, academic or sports pursuit approved by Scholastic Inc. Winner may also choose $2,500 cash payment. An approved pursuit costing less than $2,500 must be verified by bona fide invoice and presented to Scholastic Inc. prior to 7/31/95 to receive the cash difference. One hundred First Prizes each a selection by Scholastic Inc. of BSC videos, Ann Martin books, t-shirts and games. Estimated value each $10.00. Sweepstakes void where prohibited, subject to all federal, state, provincial, local laws and regulations. Odds of winning depend on the number of entries received. Prize winners are notified by mail. Grand Prize winners and parent/legal guardian are mailed a Affidavit of Eligibility/ Liability/ Publicity/Release to be executed and returned within 14 days of its date or an alternate winner may be drawn. Only one prize allowed a person or household. Taxes on prize, expenses incurred outside of prize provision and any injury, loss or damages incurred by acceptance and use of prizes are the sole responsibility of the winners and their parent/legal guardian. Prizes cannot be exchanged, transferred or cashed. Scholastic Inc. reserves the right to substitute prizes of like value if any offered are unavailable and to use the names and likenesses of prize winners without further compensation for advertising and promotional use. Prizes that are unclaimed or undelivered to winner's address remain the property of Scholastic Inc. For a Winners List, please send a stamped, addressed envelope to THE BSC REMEMBERS Sweepstakes Winners, Smiley Promotion Inc., 271 Madison Avenue, #802, New York, N.Y. 10016 after 11/30/94. Residents of Washington state may omit return stamp.

Create Your Own Mystery Stories!

THE BABY-SITTERS CLUB®

MYSTERY GAME!

WHO: Boyfriend   **WHY:** Romance

WHAT: Phone Call   **WHERE:** Dance

Use the special Mystery Case card to pick WHO did it, WHAT was involved, WHY it happened and WHERE it happened. Then dial secret words on your Mystery Wheels to add to the story! Travel around the special Stoneybrook map gameboard to uncover your friends' secret word clues! Finish four baby-sitting jobs and find out all the words to win. Then have everyone join in to tell the story!